THE LIGHT CALIBURN

Nimue   Pelleas

BY JAKE FROST

Dedication

For Cecelia, who told me: "You don't always have to research everything first, sometimes you just write it."

and

For Luke, who told me: "You have to invest the time in research if you want to find the good stuff."

You were both right!

What if the legends of King Arthur
have survived for a thousand years because
of the secret they hold, hidden in plain sight?

What if the legends have survived for a thousand
years because they're true?

St. Michael's Tower, Glastonbury Tor, United Kingdom, where Avalon was located

The Light of Caliburn

From Alette's research notes:

When the men from the dragon-prowed ships came, King Arthur had but a small band of knights from the Round Table to meet them in combat, while the host of the enemy was so vast that to see the shafts of their spears when they were arrayed for battle was like looking on the Forest of Caledon.

Yet defend the land King Arthur must, and defend the land King Arthur would.

Merlin came to him as King Arthur was preparing for battle and said: "My King, do not take the great sword Caliburn from its sheath unless you have the utmost need. Only then, at your final extremity, draw the mighty weapon. And then, give your utmost."

King Arthur heeded the words of Merlin, his great friend and advisor, and went into battle at the head of his knights with his spear Ron in hand, which had been crafted by the old wizard Wygar, and the sword Caliburn in its sheath at his side.

With his knights riding behind him King Arthur charged the enemy and crashed into their ranks like thunder! Heavy were the blows dealt by King Arthur and the noble Knights of the Round Table! Valiantly they fought to defend the realm! Many of the enemy were slain.

But King Arthur and his knights were too few in number. Compared to the horde of the dragon-men they were like a pebble dropped in the midst of a great sea. As many as King Arthur and the Knights of the Round Table cut down, still more closed around them.

The weight of the enemy's numbers began to grind upon them and the tide of battle began to go against them. Many of their company were slain and the enemy pressed them harder and harder. At last King Arthur and those of his knights that still remained were surrounded on all sides. Still, Arthur fought on fiercely, smiting before him and behind him.

Then King Arthur's horse was slain beneath him and Arthur toppled to the ground as his steed fell!

When the enemy saw Arthur go down, they were filled with glee and went into a mad frenzy of bloodlust, seeking to finish off the Britons once and for all. Arthur's remaining knights managed to raise him again to his feet amid the rain of blows from the dragon-men. Then, in the midst of the ravening dragon-men and on the verge of being submerged beneath the great multitude of the enemy, when all seemed lost, King Arthur put his strong hand to the hilt of Caliburn.

Arthur drew Caliburn from its sheath, and lo! A great light burst from the blade and shone across the land!

The dragon-men stood still, blinded in the radiance of Caliburn as King Arthur raised the shining blade!

The commonfolk saw The Light of Caliburn from where they lay in hiding, for when first the dragon-men came a-harrowing, the people of the land had run to the forests and wild places seeking hidey-holes. Now they beheld The Light of Caliburn from the pits and shadows where they cowered and they saw their King on the point of being crushed beneath the dark sea of their enemies, and their fear turned to wrath.

"This is our King!" they cried. "This is our land! For our homes, for our people, let us fight! No more will we hide! With our King this day we conquer or die!"

The commonfolk took up staves of wood from the forests and stones from the fields and charged the enemy with a mighty battle shout! Furious was their onslaught, so intent were they on sending as many of the dragon-men off to hell as they could! And their peasant arms were strong! They smote with stave and stone and broke many a dragon-man's bone! Skulls were cracked and brains were splattered and much dragon blood was spilled! Many a haughty invader in his shining armor was laid low by the powerful blows of the peasants in their rough home-spun woolens! The glittering thanes from across the bitter sea now trembled before the might of the English folk!

Together with Arthur, their King, the people of the land slew so many of the invaders that the dead could not be counted and none was left of that vaunted host that came to kill and plunder, and any few who escaped fled in terror from those they had come to prey upon, trying to save their cursed lives!

King Arthur and his people were victorious, and never again feared the dragon-men, but from that day forward were ever ready to crush their enemy in battle wherever they might be met.

See *Le Morte D'Arthur*, by Sir Thomas Malory (circa 1450 A.D.)

The ruins of Vortigern's tower on Dinys Emrys, Wales, where Merlin slew two dragons (see "Merlin and the Tower of the Dragons," page 41)

Table of Contents

Chapter 1

A Hidden Treasure

From Alette's research notes:

Arthur laid his hand to the sword in the stone and drew it out while Sir Ector looked on in awe.

Sir Ector had raised Arthur since Arthur was a baby, without ever knowing who he was, ever since Merlin brought Arthur to Sir Ector's gate in secret one dark night when Arthur was still an infant and delivered him to Sir Ector.

Now Sir Ector knelt before Arthur.

"Why do you kneel?" asked Arthur, confused.

"Because you are King of this land," answered Sir Ector.

"King?" asked Arthur. "Why should I be King?"

"Because God wills it," answered Sir Ector.

See *Le Morte D'Arthur*, by Sir Thomas Malory (circa 1450 A.D.)

It was a very odd occurrence.

Geo looked down at what he held in his hands and

could not believe what he saw. But there it was: a thin case covered with beaten gold, with a design worked into its overleaf closure of a tree in full leaf, rich with fruit, with a flaming sword before it, and two words, one on each side of the tree: *Nimue* on one side, *Pelleas* on the other.

The gold gleamed in the sunlight.

It was gorgeous.

And he had just found it in the old voyaguer desk which for years he'd used for *plein air* painting.

The voyaguer desk was a portable writing desk used by the fur traders back in the days when they canoed the rivers and trekked the forests of the New World seeking fortune and adventure. The desks were slim and light enough to be borne on the back as they were carried across continents traversed by foot and paddle, but strong enough to withstand the hardships of the frontier. Writing implements—paper, ink, quills—were stored in a compartment beneath the lid, while the lid itself served as the writing surface. With such simple instruments as these were the financial records of the vast fur trading empires kept, whose fortunes reshaped continental Europe.

Geo had received the voyaguer desk long ago as a gift from an old man cleaning out his cabin in the backcountry of Michigan's Upper Peninsula before selling and leaving Copper Country for good. The old man's name was Ron Wygar, and Geo had known him for years, making a point of stopping at Mr. Wygar's cabin as he travelled the wild regions of the Upper Peninsula on his painting excursions. Whenever he was near he'd check-in to see how Mr. Wygar was getting along, offer a helping hand, and listen to Mr. Wygar's stories of Copper Country. Mr. Wygar loved the history of the Northern forests and delighted in sharing their lore with Geo, especially stories of George Northrup, "The Man that Draws the Handcart," because Geo shared a name with the famous frontiersman renowned for his incredible toughness and great kindness. The frontiersman had gained his sobriquet by walking across the country and into the wilderness carrying his few possessions in a handcart which he pulled, since he had no horse. Geo's full name was George Northrup, "Geo" (pronounced *G-O*, or *Gee-Oh*) was the nickname he'd acquired in his school days growing up along the rocky coasts of Superior in the Keweenaw Peninsula. A teacher once wrote *"Geo."* on the board as an abbreviation for George, and "Geo" had stuck with him ever since. Even after years away from the Upper Peninsula during his military service, when he came back he was still "Geo" on Copper Island.

Except with Mr. Wygar. Mr. Wygar always insisted on using Geo's full name of *George*, saying it was too noble not to.

Among Mr. Wygar's eclectic mix of interests was a love for the voyaguers, the chivalric "Knights of the North" who had plied the great lakes with their enormous Montreal canoes, and particularly the voyaguer songs. Mr. Wygar was an accomplished musician and a fine singer with dozens of voyaguer songs in his repertoire. When Mr. Wygar gave the desk to Geo he told him it was a genuine relic of the fur trade, a part of the tradition of the North, and that it ought to remain in the lands of the Great Lakes where it belonged. He wanted Geo to have it, and Geo had kept it ever since.

Geo didn't know where the desk originally came from, or how old it was, but it was sturdy, and had served him well painting out in the hills and forests of the Upper Peninsula. And in all the years he'd used the voyaguer desk he never suspected the secret it held.

There were legendary stories of the strange treasures discovered in the wilds around the Great Lakes: hoards of ancient coins from civilizations across the sea, caches of swords and armor, statues and figurines of unknown origin, stones inscribed with Viking runes, tablets carved with hieroglyphs that had never been deciphered, all manner of unexplainable antiquities.

And there were mysteries like the ancient stone forts left by unknown builders that were scattered all across the islands and shores of Superior, or the ring of stones arranged in astronomical alignments that lay on the 45th Parallel on Beaver Island in Lake Michigan, corresponding with the Medicine Wheel in Wyoming that was also located on the 45th Parallel. There were lost treasure ships like *The Griffon* which had set sail upon the treacherous waters of the Great Lakes never to be seen again.

But Geo had never heard of anything like this.

He was in an alpine meadow of The Cliffs, a range of mountains in the Keweenaw Peninsula, where he'd come to paint. Geo was a professional oil painter specializing in the rugged landscapes of the Great Lakes region. Hiking to remote corners of the wilderness to capture the Keweenaw's beauty in oils was one of his favorite things about life as an artist. He was tall and tan, lean and solid, with dark brown hair and clear, brown eyes. He weighed 195 pounds, fifteen pounds more than when he'd enlisted in the army a dozen years before. And every pound he'd added since was muscle earned with axe and paddle and hiking under a load.

He'd loved the military, but his passion for art had grown during his years in boots. He started taking a sketch box with him everywhere he went, drawing and painting in every spare moment. When Geo learned that Bob Ross, the famous television painter, had begun his art career while on active duty in the military, Ross became an inspiration for Geo. Finally, after years of honing his art, Geo decided the time had come to go for it himself.

And for six years now he'd made it work. He'd found a level of success that offered stability, even a degree of comfort, though fame and riches eluded him.

That was all right. He loved painting and he loved the outdoors, and he'd seen his mastery of his chosen art grow tremendously over the past six years. He counted himself blessed every morning he woke up and got to head out into the woods and hills or tramp the awe-inspiring coasts of the Upper Peninsula, set up his easel, and try again to create something beautiful.

And it had been out in the wilderness, working on a painting, that it happened. He'd been sitting on a folding stool, his palette in held one hand, when he

15

leaned back to consider his canvass and reached into the voyaguer desk with his other hand to get a brush. Without taking his eyes from the canvas, he felt around inside the desk for the brush, just as he'd done a thousand times before. But this time his fingers pressed something that yielded. There was a click, and a panel in the bottom of the desk popped up.

Surprised, Geo set aside his palette to investigate. He saw the bottom panel askew inside the desk and beneath it was a hollow space, a secret compartment. Inside, something glittered. He felt around the edges of the bottom panel and lifted it out. And there was the golden case.

Now he held it in his hands and examined it in the sunlight.

Even more peculiar than the case itself was a strange feeling that crept over him, a premonition, that this was more than one spectacular find: it was a turning point. He sensed that somehow his life was about to change forever.

The case itself seemed charged with energy that tingled into his fingers as he held it.

For the rest of his life, Geo would always remember that moment, that feeling of being on the point of a fulcrum, poised between what had been, and what was about to be, between what he had always known and the mystery that lay ahead. And always, even years and years later, he remembered that first feeling of power surging into his fingertips.

It almost felt as if the case *wanted* to be opened, that it *longed* to be opened.

And not just to be opened, but opened *by him.* Somehow he knew that he was meant to find the case, to find it and open it.

The sensation of pent-up energy, bristling and urging to be released, grew.

Wondering what was about to happen, Geo opened the case.

Carving of King Arthur on the Modena Cathedral located in Modena, Italy

Chapter 2

The Book of Merlin

From Alette's research notes:

> *Arthur became shining bright, his strength immense, and he moved like lighting. He smashed through shield and helm and armor, felling a foe with every blow. No man could stand against him.*

See *The History of the Kings of Britain*, by Geoffrey of Monmouth (circa 1130 A.D.)

With his fingers tingling where they touched the case, Geo lifted its cover and saw within a slim volume of vellum pages stitched together along one side. He took it out and read the hand-written cover: *The Book of Merlin*.

Geo opened the book and when he lifted its cover a torrent of power burst from it, rushing all around him, enveloping him as it swept outwards in waves of energy. The air was filled with a shimmer of sparkling radiance as power poured from the book. Within the rush of energy Geo had the sensation of being caught in the mighty swell of an ocean current.

All the world outside the cascade of power seemed to blur and Geo could hear nothing beyond its crackle of energy.

He looked at the book held in his hands and began to read the first page:

> *I, Blaise, have faithfully taken down in this Book of Merlin the words imparted to me by Merlin, my famous fellow servant, who calls me master, but with whom I am blessed to serve.*

Next to this was a marginal note written in another hand, which read: "Blessed Blaise saved my mother twice before I was born, first and most importantly her life eternal, and second, her life temporal, while she still carried me in her womb, and thereby he saved my life also, so Master indeed I call him, and rightly so." Then the handwriting of Blaise continued:

> *Merlin bids me give this warning: they will come. Prepare for battle. The Spartoi, enemies of Merlin and all mankind, seek always to destroy and consume the dust. With the opening of this book they will feel the release of its power, and they will come.*
> *Arm yourself with the gifts of Creation. You will not have much time.*
> *Invoke the Genesis Cycles that you may*

19

conquer the dragons.

    The First Cycle imparts great power but exacts a great price. Use it only as a last resort, at the hour of greatest need.

Geo turned the page and read on the top of the next: *The First Cycle*. Below, the page contained only a few words, which Geo read aloud:

Before moon or sun there was The Light
Instill in me its burning might

    The energy pouring from the open book swirled and eddied and began to organize itself into forms and patterns, no longer raging about him in a wild storm, but now weaving itself into designs. He caught only glimpses of the constantly shifting patterns, for as soon as he could discern one it was already breaking up to reform again into something new. Then the power began whirling inward, converging on him, until finally it flowed into him, penetrating his skin, pouring into his muscles, into his bones, so he felt its shifting patterns rippling through his body. Suddenly the power gripped him entirely. For a moment he was rigid, locked in its grasp, and a white-hot fire burned through every fiber of his being.

    Just as suddenly, he was released.

    Geo stood wondering what had just happened. He closed *The Book of Merlin* and the outward rushing of power cut off instantly with the shutting of the book's cover.

He heard again the sounds of the forest and meadow.

Then Geo began to feel energy welling within him. His skin prickled, his vision shifted, and suddenly a pulse of Light burst from his body and blasted outward. For a moment, everything was frozen as The Light flashed over it—birds, trees, everything The Light touched was arrested in mid-motion, as if it were momentarily suspended in time, or as if he himself had slipped outside the flow of time.

Geo looked around with wonder. Within every living thing he saw a burning Light. It was in the trees and grasses, in the squirrels on branches and rabbits crouching beneath bushes.

And though all things were held motionless by The Light, the burning inner Light within each thing still danced like a bright tongue of flickering fire, brilliant and beautiful. He could easily pick out each little creature where it hid by the Light that burned within it. And there, far out in the woods, was a great stag with an incredible, breathtaking Light burning within its deep chest. The great stag seemed to be returning Geo's far-seeing gaze, looking straight at him across the forest.

Then the pulse of Light passed onward, flashing over the meadow and forest, out into the sky and off over Lake Superior. Everything which had been suspended and held still in The Light was released. The forest and meadow exploded into motion all around him. Birds shot into the air, squirrels chattered and ran, rabbits leapt, and the great stag far out in the woods started into a sprint.

Geo felt a strength in his body he had never known. He threw his head back and laughed for pure joy at the sensation of life and vitality coursing through him. He held his hands up and clenched his fists just to feel their might and saw that his body glowed with a bright luminescence.

He looked out again and spotted the stag darting away through the forest. Geo watched the dancing of its magnificent inner Light and then, without thinking, purely for the thrill of feeling the new power of his muscles at work, took off after it.

The jolt of speed was shocking as he sprang forward and raced through the meadow and into the forest, moving so fast that the air against his face was like a gale and threw his hair flying back as he charged over the ground.

The stag had disappeared from view. Ahead Geo saw a great, rocky cliff. He veered toward it to gain a vantage point above the forest from which to spy the stag. The cliff face was almost sheer but Geo scaled it in seconds.

From the summit he scanned the forest. Below, all ablaze with the inner fire revealed by The Light, unbroken forest stretched to the shores of Lake Superior, where, from the swarms of fish swimming beneath its sparkling waves, hundreds of flaming sparks burned brighter even than the flashes of sunlight reflected on the lake's restless surface.

It was all so beautiful.

Laughter shook him again. A great stone sat atop

the cliff and out of sheer exuberance Geo picked it up and flung it over Superior. He watched it spin through the air in a high arc, reach its zenith, then start back downwards to finally splash far out in the water.

The flaming sparks of the fish streaked away beneath the waves, darting from the stone suddenly crashing into their watery world.

But as Geo stood gazing over all the wonder before him, he became aware of a gnawing pain inside himself. He could feel The Light, the power, burning him from within, consuming him. The longer The Light burned, the more it ached.

He let The Light ebb away, watching his hands dim as the power drained from him. When the last of The Light had left him, he collapsed on the cliff top, panting, sore and exhausted. He was so hungry it hurt.

He lay a long time, feeling his heart hammering in his chest and trying to catch his breath while he watched the clouds float by overhead.

At last he pulled himself slowly up into a sitting position and looked out over the forest. Without The Light burning within him, he could no longer see the inner flame of the trees or animals, only the canopy of the forest stretching away, and there, far out, the clearing where he'd been painting.

He was surprised how far away it was. He hadn't realized he'd covered so much distance so quickly.

He stood, and his limbs trembled, still shaky with exhaustion. He sat down again.

How am I going to get back? Geo wondered.

Without The Light there was no way he could reach

the meadow before nightfall, but he didn't think he could bear it again, certainly not now.

I'll rest longer, Geo thought. *When I get some strength back, I'll try The Light again.*

He settled himself and concentrated on his breathing. He marked the shifting of shadows as the sun made its way across the sky while he waited and gave himself time to recover. The wind blowing off Superior was cool on the cliff top.

When he felt he'd regained as much strength as he could, Geo stood and readied himself. He began tentatively, trying to kindle just a little of The Light, and found he could control its intensity. He drew it forth gradually so that the great pulse of Light didn't burst from him. As The Light burned hotter and brighter, he could see the dancing flames beginning to emerge within living things, like candle flames shining faintly through a veil. And there, amid the trees at the base of the cliff, Geo saw the great stag again, recognizing it by its magnificent inner Light.

But he had no thought of chasing it now. He could already feel the burning of The Light consuming him. He had to get back to the clearing while he still could.

With the strength and speed of The Light, Geo scaled down the cliff and raced off through the trees, heading for the clearing and the trail leading to his Jeep.

The Light seared through him, wracking his body with pain. He began letting it fade even as he ran. His strength and speed slackened as The Light drained from him, but so did the pain of its inner burning. By

24

the time he reached the clearing and collapsed on the ground next to the voyaguer desk he had let the last of The Light extinguish entirely and he was utterly spent.

He lay panting on the ground and smiled.

That had been just the First Cycle of *The Book of Merlin*. He wondered what else awaited him within its pages.

Statue of Saint Michael the Archangel atop the spire of Mont Saint-Michel

Chapter 3

A Sudden Chill

From Alette's research notes:

He was tested by the sword and found a man capable for war.

See *The Life of Merlin*, by Geoffrey of Monmouth (circa 1150 A.D.)

From Alette's research notes:

When Merlin looked at the beggar where he sat with hand outstretched for alms he shook his head, for by his arts Merlin could see that untold wealth lay at the beggar's feet, in a great hoard of gold and silver buried in the very ground upon which the beggar sat day after day, begging in his tattered rags.

See *The Life of Merlin*, by Geoffrey of Monmouth (circa 1150 A.D.)

Geo lay on the grass, aching all over.

He remembered the punishment his body had taken on military field exercises in Hawaii, when they'd crawled under barbed wire strung over the sharp, jagged stones of old lava flows while machine gun fire rattled overhead. He'd been sore for days afterwards.

He remembered fights from his boxing days that left every inch of his body feeling bruised and battered.

But he'd never felt anything like this.

Holding the golden case containing *The Book of Merlin*, Geo thought: *I can't believe I've been carrying this around all these years and never knew it was here.*

The voyaguer desk had been with him on painting excursions all over the Keweenaw Peninsula. He'd had it the time when, in a meadow much like this, he'd felt a chill creep over him. The hairs on his arms stood on end and he became aware of a presence.

He turned to see a bear staring at him from the edge of the forest, and not with a look of curiosity, but of intent, the look of a hunter sighting prey.

Geo was alone on Brockway Mountain and he'd left his gun in the Jeep back at the trail head.

The bear started shuffling out of the trees toward him.

Geo knew bears can sprint faster than a horse and climb trees like a squirrel.

There was no chance of outrunning it, and it would be worse than foolish to try. To a bear flight only signaled weakness, easy pickings to be readily had.

Years before, when Geo worked a summer at

Glacier National Park, an old ranger told him: the law of the wild is that the strong devours the weak, so be strong. The ranger said that if Geo were ever confronted by a bear he had to make himself appear as large and fearsome as possible to convince the bear that the cost of coming for him was higher than it wanted to pay. The ranger told him to pick things up and wave them over his head to enlarge his profile and scream like his life depended on it—because it did. Most battles, the ranger said, were fought in the mind—for bear and people alike. An unarmed human might be too weak to attack a bear's body, but he could still attack a bear's mind. Make it fear, the ranger told him, and the bear will defeat itself.

When Geo stood alone that day on Brockway Mountain with the bear lumbering toward him and adrenaline flooding his body, his mind went calm and he remembered the old ranger's words.

The thing closest to hand was the voyaguer desk.

Geo grabbed it, held it above his head, and roared at the bear.

It stopped.

It looked at Geo, swinging its massive head side to side, hesitating, assessing.

Geo roared again, his body taught as a bow string.

The bear was enormous, easily five hundred pounds. It opened its gigantic maw, revealing huge yellow fangs, and bellowed back at Geo its own determination to dominate, to kill, to feed.

But Geo had not been afraid. Instead, he became enraged. He roared right back and knew, with a certainty like cold steel inside him, that he would fight. Come what may, he would fight. If he had to, he would sell his life as dearly as possible.

The next moments were forever etched in Geo's memory by the sharp edge where life and death meet. He and the bear each stood their ground, testing, challenging, pitting will against will as they roared back and forth at each other.

The bear broke first.

It lowered its head and averted its eyes. Then it turned and hurried back into the trees.

Geo remained where he was a few minutes more, his blood tingling from the encounter. Then he calmly put the voyaguer desk down, collected his things and stowed them, and walked back to his Jeep.

As he thought back to that episode, Geo laughed when he remembered Alette's reaction when he told her what happened. She had been so mad. Her father was a French-Canadian hunter and trapper in the wilderness on the other side of Lake Superior. He'd raised Alette in the woods with French and the wild as her first languages.

And she still has traces of both accents, Geo thought with a smile.

Alette could read the weather by the smell of the wind, track an animal through the brush like she was following a trail marked on a map, and live off the land in any season.

She knew the wilderness and knew how dangerous the northern forests could be. She also knew how absorbed Geo became in his painting, focusing on a canvas to the point of being oblivious to all else around him. She'd seen it accompanying him on his painting adventures. She was a chemistry professor at Michigan Tech and loved coming out with Geo when he hiked into the backcountry to paint. She relished the time outdoors, relished the time with him, and was glad for the chance to escape for a while from the lab and lecture hall where she spent so many hours. She would bring a picnic basket and her guitar and sit on a blanket playing and singing the old folk songs she loved and reciting poems from memory while Geo painted. And when they were heading out to remote areas, Alette never forgot her gun. It would always be right next to her on the picnic blanket as she sang and strummed her guitar.

Bullets and melody, Geo thought, *they both capture something of her spirit.*

Alette had to see this. If anyone could make sense of it, it would be Alette, with her scientist's mind and poet's soul.

Suddenly Geo shivered. All at once he felt as if he'd been plunged into deep, cool shadow. He looked up at the sky. It was clear and blue without a cloud to be seen. But he still felt a chill.

He got up.

It was time to go.

Chapter 4

Alette

From Alette's research notes:

Merlin could not always be with King Arthur for he had much to do in other places, some far away and wild, across land and sea. Often would Merlin come and go, and sometimes his errands kept him long away.

So Merlin trained the maiden Nimue that she might help Arthur when he could not be present, and he shared with her knowledge of his arts.

Nimue became Lady of the Lake and came often to King Arthur's court and was a great support to him in all he did, especially after Merlin went away the last time. Indeed, Nimue saved King Arthur's life more than once. It was Nimue, too, who saved Arthur at the end, and it was she who brought him into Avalon.

See *Le Morte D'Arthur*, by Sir Thomas Malory (circa 1450 A.D.)

From Alette's research notes:

The Lady of the Lake was trained by Merlin. He

shared his knowledge and arts with her, and she made a book in which she wrote all that Merlin taught her.

See *The Story of Merlin*, by Anonymous (circa 1215 A.D.)

From Alette's research notes:

Merlin prepared in advance what would be needed by those he enlisted in the war against the dragons. For Galahad, it was years and years before that Merlin forged the great weapons that would be used by that peerless knight. Merlin placed them in a wooden vessel and set the vessel on a course so that it would cross Galahad's path when the precise time came for him to have them. Galahad found them just as he was about to embark on his quest and used them to achieve victory, though only after great struggle.

See *Le Morte D'Arthur*, by Sir Thomas Malory (circa 1450 A.D.)

From Alette's research notes:

Merlin wrote down such things as would aid others in completing the tasks allotted to them, for he knew well that each man must do his own work or that work will go undone in this world, and he left his writings where they would be found in the time of their need.

See *The Story of Merlin*, by Anonymous (circa 1215 A.D.)

The odd chill clung to Geo and he knew it was time to go.

He packed-up his painting gear and hiked back down the trail to the Jeep. He stowed his easel and other equipment in the back but set the voyaguer desk and golden case on the front seat next to him. He started the drive home, aching, exhausted, and ravenously hungry.

It was a long way over bumpy dirt tracks before he reached pavement, and further after that before he picked-up cell coverage. When he finally did, he pulled over and texted Alette.

Honey, I found something you've got to see. How about dinner tonight at my place?

After he sent the text he started driving again. He knew better than to wait for an answer. Alette usually kept her phone in a desk drawer, turned off, to prevent distractions while she worked in the lab. So he waited, and wondered what she would make of *The Book of Merlin* as he drove the long way home.

Geo's house was on Copper Island on a high ridge overlooking Portage Lake in Hancock, Michigan. The sun was low in the sky by the time he pulled into his driveway. The Bridge cast a long shadow over the water. The Portage Lake Lift Bridge, known simply as "the Bridge" to locals, spans Portage Lake, connecting Hancock and Copper Island to the rest of the Keweenaw Peninsula. The Bridge is the largest double-decker lift bridge in the world, capable of rising 100 feet above the water's surface to allow the big ships carrying ore and timber to pass beneath it.

Geo got out of the Jeep and paused to watch sunlight sparkle on the water. Across the lake lights were coming on in Houghton, the town on the other side of Portage Lake. An eagle swooped through the sky. Geo watched it until it flew out of sight. He loved Copper Country.

When the eagle disappeared from view Geo got the golden case and voyaguer desk from the Jeep and went in. He put them on the dining room table and walked through sliding doors to the deck at the back of the house. Perched atop the ridge, the deck offered magnificent views of the lake and Bridge and the glowing lights of Houghton beyond.

He started a fire in the grill and went back into the kitchen to prepare steaks and wrap potatoes in aluminum foil for baking directly on the coals. He took out one steak for himself, one for Alette, then added another for himself.

Once the fire in the grill had burned down and the coals were glowing red, he put on the steaks and potatoes, then was busy going back and forth between the kitchen and deck getting everything ready for an outdoor dinner. He brought out the golden case containing *The Book of Merlin* and set it on the deck table to show Alette when she arrived.

When the salad was made and the wine poured, all was ready.

His phone beeped. It was a text from Alette: *Sounds great. Are you home? I'll be right over.*

He texted back: *Steaks are on the grill.*

He smiled. He always did when he knew he'd be seeing her soon.

He went to the grill to turn the meat and gazed out over the water. The sun was a deep red, sinking toward the horizon. He turned the meat again and just as the steaks were done he heard Alette's car pull into the driveway.

He was putting the food on the plates when she walked around the corner of the house.

He looked up and saw her, golden hair shimmering in the light of the evening sun. She was slim and willowy and moved with the grace of waves on a moonlit bay.

"You look beautiful," he told her.

"Thank you," she said, smiling as she climbed the steps up to the deck. "I love hearing that from you."

He gave her a kiss and led her by the hand to the table.

"You know how to win a girl's heart," Alette said, "with sweet words and red meat!"

"Don't forget the wine," Geo said.

"Ahh," she sighed, "with wine you get to keep the heart forever."

Geo laughed.

"Come on, let's pray," he said. "I'm starving."

"I can see," Alette said. "Two steaks? How far did you hike today? And how was the painting?"

"I went way further than I intended," Geo answered, "and the painting was fine until I got interrupted."

Alette raised an eyebrow. "Interrupted?" she asked. "By what?"

"Let's pray," Geo urged. "I'll tell you while we eat."

They folded their hands and said grace. While they were praying Alette saw the golden case on the table. She looked at him with surprise.

When they finished grace she said, "That's beautiful. What is it?"

"That's the interruption," Geo answered. "It's what I texted you about."

"Where did you get it?" Alette asked.

"I found it in my old voyaguer desk, inside a secret compartment in the bottom."

"Are you serious?" she asked, reaching out to pick-up the case.

Her fingertips came in contact with the case's gleaming surface and reflexively her hand jerked back.

"Did you feel it?" Geo asked.

"What is it?" she asked.

"I have no idea," Geo said. "Energy. Power. If anyone can figure it out, it's you. But be careful. Inside is a book, *The Book of Merlin*, and the tingle that comes through the case is nothing compared to what's released when you open the book itself. In fact, you shouldn't open it here. We'll go into the mountains tomorrow and you can open it there."

"Why? What happens when you open the book?" Alette asked.

In answer, Geo held up his hand and let The Light begin to burn faintly within him. His hand began to glow and Alette's eyes widened.

Geo let The Light fade again. Even that little bit had been painful after the burning of The Light that afternoon.

"That's what the book calls *The First Cycle*," Geo said. "Power came out of the book when I opened it and then when I read the words of *The First Cycle* it somehow triggered or directed the power so it went into me. It gives incredible strength and speed."

Alette reached out her hand again and carefully picked up the golden case.

While she examined it Geo turned to his food. His hand trembled from The Light as he held his fork.

Alette turned the case over front and back, studying it. "Gold, over a hard subsurface," she said, "probably metal, possibly a hard wood. Beautiful design of a fruit laden tree, burning sword, and two words: Nimue and Pelleas. Any idea what they mean?"

"None," Geo said. "I just got back and started dinner. I haven't had a chance to try deciphering anything yet."

Alette opened the case and carefully slid out *The Book of Merlin*.

She held it up and read the title aloud. But to Geo's surprise, she read it in French.

French was her first language, and he'd begun picking-up French from her, but she usually spoke English with him.

"Why in French?" he asked.

"It's written in French," she said.

"What?" Geo asked.

Alette turned the book to show its cover to Geo.

The words on the cover were now written in French.

"It was in English when I read it earlier today," Geo said, bewildered. "Can I see that?"

Alette handed him the book.

When it was back in Geo's hands and Alette no longer touched it, the ink on the cover began to blur. The edges of the writing became fuzzy, the ink dissolved into liquidity, then started to flow like watercolor paint bleeding across wet paper. It swam in swirling puddles over the vellum cover and began to reform itself, resolving again into letters that once more spelled the title in English.

They both looked up from the book and their eyes met. Geo shook his head in amazement and handed it back to Alette.

When Alette held the book the words on the cover again blurred, the ink swirled, and the writing reformed into French.

"What is this thing?" Geo asked.

"Amazing," Alette said. "Besides that, I don't know. Yet."

Geo smiled. That was Alette.

He went back to his steaks and potatoes while she

continued examining the book. By the time Geo finished eating the sky was dusky and the shadow of the Bridge was a dark purple over the charcoal colors of the water. There was a chill in the air. Geo felt drowsy, but Alette was still absorbed in *The Book of Merlin*.

"How about coffee?" he asked.

Alette looked up from the book and smiled.

"Yes please," she said. "It's getting cold, shall we go in?"

"Yes, let's," Geo answered. "I'll start a fire."

They went in and Geo arranged logs in the fireplace while Alette settled herself in the easy chair across from it with the book.

"I've heard of Merlin, of course," she said, "but Nimue and Pelleas I don't know. They might be names, also. And these symbols, the tree and the sword, what do they mean?"

"When I opened the book," Geo said, striking a match and holding it to crumpled newspaper placed amid the kindling, "the first page said there is a battle with the Spartoi, whatever that means, and that the Spartoi will come when the book is opened. It also said you could use the *Cycles* of the book to conquer dragons."

The fire caught and flames licked up. Wood crackled and flickering shadows sprang up around the room. The warmth of the fire felt good to Geo's aching muscles.

He went to make coffee, adding cream and sugar to Alette's the way she always liked it, leaving his own black.

He brought the coffee out and handed Alette her cup.

"Thank you," she said. Geo sat on the couch across from her and took a big drink from his cup. Sighing with appreciation, he placed the cup on the end table next to the couch and lay down on the couch with his head on a pillow.

"The first place to start," Alette said, thinking aloud, "will be with the text once I can open the book, though I see what you mean about not opening it here. This thing is full of surprises."

Geo chuckled and closed his eyes.

"But along with the text," Alette continued, "the name Merlin points to Arthurian legend as a source for possible clues, and Spartoi is such a distinctive word it should be a good place to begin searching. Then there would be a physical examination of the book, the case, the desk and its secret compartment . . ."

Geo listened with his eyes closed as Alette outlined her campaign of investigation. This is what he knew she would do: analyze, research, discover. She was an explorer, a finder of answers, a mapper of the uncharted.

He loved that about her. He loved to see her mind at work. And he knew that once she seized on a question she would pursue it to its final end, just as she did in her scientific research, performing experiment after experiment until she unraveled whatever riddle of nature she was studying.

The last thing he remembered hearing before he fell asleep was Alette saying, "Nimue and Pelleas . . ."

Merlin and the Tower of the Dragons

From Alette's research notes:

In the days when Vortigern was High King of Britain he sought out Merlin. Vortigern was attempting to build a tower as his strong citadel, but the tower would not stand. During the day, stone was laid upon stone and the walls rose. But each night, when dark came, the stones would all be cast down in a confusion of chaos.

Merlin came to Vortigern and told him: "O King, your tower will not stand because you attempt to build on a foundation of dragons. Thus it ends always in chaos and ruin."

The King and all his court were puzzled by these words. "We see no dragons," they said.

Merlin answered: "That is because they are hidden, deep, deep. If you dig under the ground you will find a cavern in which is a lake, and under the water of the lake you will find two large stones, and under those stones you will find two dragons. It is they who overthrow each night what has been built in the day."

"How then can we build?" asked the King.

"First you must slay the dragons," answered Merlin.

"How can we slay the dragons?" asked the King.

"With the light," said Merlin. "Root them out, dig into the earth, drain the pool, overturn the rocks, and drag the dragons into the light."

So the King ordered his men to do as Merlin said, and as they dug into the earth they found the cavern with a lake, just as Merlin had said. They drained the water of the lake and found two great stones, just as Merlin had said. They turned over the stones and found beneath them two dragons, just as Merlin had said. The dragons were sleeping, each huge, hideous, and disgusting to behold, and terribly strong.

The men threw ropes around the necks of the sleeping dragons and hauled them out of their secret hiding places into the light. When the light fell upon them, the dragons were enraged and lashed out and attacked one another, and in their madness the dragons slew each other and were destroyed.

All who saw it were amazed. Then Merlin said to the King: "Build, and now will your tower stand." And the King built, and his tower stood.

See *The Story of Merlin*, by Anonymous (circa 1215 A.D.); see *Brut*, by Layamon (circa 1190 A.D.); see *Roman de Brute*, by Wace (circa 1150 A.D.).

Chapter 5

They Will Come Soon

From Alette's research notes:

Cadmus slew the dragon. But then from the seed of the dragon's teeth came the Spartoi, for when the dragon's teeth were sown in the earth, the Spartoi sprang out of the dust. The Spartoi were dragon-men, mad, violent, full of wrath and bloodshed.

When Cadmus looked and beheld the Spartoi in the field, all armed and menacing, he was greatly alarmed and picked up a stone and cast it at the Spartoi. The stone struck a Spartoi, and when the Spartoi was hit he turned immediately to the Spartoi nearest him and lashed out with his sword. That Spartoi then raged in violence at those around him, and in this way all the Spartoi were soon slaying one another so that the field was red with blood. For the Spartoi, even though they opened their hearts to the dragon, still are men of dust like Adam, and mortal like all of Adam's sons. For the Spartoi are indeed men, but men who have allowed the dragon's poison, represented by the seed of the dragon's tooth, to grow within them, and it is that

*which makes them mad and destroys all
reason and drives them always to consume
flesh of dust.*

See the Greek legend of Cadmus and the
Spartoi

Geo opened his eyes. Sunlight streamed in through
a crack in the curtains. He stretched, felt his muscles
tighten and relax, and yawned.

"Welcome back to the world," Alette said and Geo
turned to see her.

"Good morning," he said.

"More like good afternoon," Alette answered.
"You've been out for . . ." she looked at her watch, "the
last fourteen hours."

He was laying on the couch still wearing his clothes
from the night before, but a blanket covered him and
his boots were off. He wiggled his toes in their
stockings.

"When I couldn't wake you," Alette said, "I tried to
make you comfortable. Your boots are by the couch."

"Thanks," he said. "I feel a lot better. Wait until you
try The Light. It's amazing, but it takes everything out
of you."

"Speaking of which," Alette said, "there was a news
report this morning about a strange phenomenon in
the mountains yesterday. People reported seeing an

44

intense flash of light and some sort of projectile flying into the lake."

"That was me," Geo said, sitting up. "I threw a huge rock into the water. What did the news say?"

"Only that the flash of light could be seen for miles. They checked with the Air Force and Navy but neither were holding exercises."

NASA used to conduct missile tests at the Keweenaw Rocket Range, and the Air Force and Navy both had bases on the Great Lakes. F-16's were often seen streaking over Superior from a base near Duluth, across the lake from the Keweenaw Peninsula, and the Navy ran exercises throughout the region from The Great Lakes Naval Station in Chicago.

"Did the news say anything else?" Geo asked.

"No," Alette answered, "just speculation that it could have been an atmospheric phenomenon, or related to the *Aurora Borealis*, or just one of those strange things that happens sometimes around the Great Lakes that no one can ever explain."

The chill from yesterday crept over Geo again.

"I wish it hadn't been in the news," he said.

"I found out some other things while you were sleeping," Alette said. "King Arthur also had some sort of power of Light associated with his sword Caliburn."

"I though King Arthur's sword was Excalibur?" Geo asked.

"In some stories," Alette answered, "but in the older chronicles it's called Caliburn, and they say that The Light of Caliburn would burst from the sword in a great flash and give King Arthur incredible strength and speed."

Geo gave a low whistle. "That's it exactly," he said.

"It gets more interesting," Alette said. "King Arthur got Caliburn from Merlin."

"What?"

"Yes, Merlin took Arthur to a lake where the sword was, told him about the sword and how to get it, and helped him obtain it from The Lady of the Lake. And Merlin was a dragon slayer, and he enlisted King Arthur and the Knights of the Round Table to help him in fighting dragons."

"So Merlin is the common link," Geo said, "between The Light, the book, and the dragons."

"Maybe," Alette said, "but it's confusing. There isn't one story of King Arthur that tells it all from beginning to end. Bits and pieces are sprinkled through many different tales, some only tangentially related to King Arthur and the Knights of the Round Table. But even in the realm of Arthurian literature proper, there are dozens of stories written at different times and places, going back eighteen hundred years. Each contains different parts of the whole. I've only started trying to untangle it all."

"What you've found already is amazing," Geo said.

Alette shook her head.

"Not all of it is good. I also discovered some things about the Spartoi." She paused and looked at Geo. "They were dragon-men," she said.

"What does that mean?" Geo asked.

"I'm not sure," Alette said, "but they were apparently men who had somehow taken the dragon into their hearts. It comes from Greek mythology, in the story of Cadmus, who was, by the way, the first maker of books. He was said to have invented writing and taught the secret of letters to men. And when he wasn't writing, Cadmus kept busy killing dragons."

"Like Merlin," Geo said.

Alette nodded. "And once when Cadmus killed a dragon, the dragon's teeth acted like seed. They were sown in the earth and the dragon-men, the Spartoi, grew from them. Symbolically, the earth represents man, in which the seed of the dragon is planted."

"Like Adam formed from the dust of the earth," Geo said. "Ashes to ashes and dust to dust."

"Exactly," Alette said. "The name Adam actually means earth. Then into the earth of man's heart some men allow the dragon's poison to enter, take root, and grow. They become the Spartoi, who hate, and seek to destroy all things, without reason or remorse. Even each other. Even themselves."

"And these are the dragon-men that *The Book of Merlin* says will come once the book is opened." Geo said.

"So it seems," Alette said.

"Come on," Geo said. "Let's get up into the mountains. You've done fantastic work already, but to really figure this thing out you've got to open the book."

"The Jeep's all packed and ready to go," Alette said.

Geo smiled. "Thank you," he said. "I love you."

"You should," Alette answered, and gave him a kiss.

Chapter 6

Nimue

From Alette's research notes:

The good knight Pelleas was forlorn and desolate because he loved a lady with a false heart who took his love for granted, used it when it suited her, then cast it aside. For Pelleas, though handsome and valiant, and one of the chief warriors of his age, was low-born and had risen to become a Knight of the Round Table without the aid of famous ancestry, but only by the might of his own hands and the glory of his own noble deeds. For King Arthur, who had himself been brought up in lowly circumstances as a foundling, judged a man by his deeds, not by the house he was born in.

But the false-hearted lady who abused Pelleas' love was haughty and looked down on Pelleas because he had been reared in a lowly peasant's hut.

Thus was Pelleas sorely distressed. So his friend went to Nimue, the Lady of the Lake, who was always a support to King Arthur and the Knights of the Round Table, and asked her to find some way to relieve the heart of his comrade Pelleas.

"Lead the way and I will go to him," said Nimue, "to see what I can do to help him."

So Nimue was brought to Pelleas, and when she laid eyes on him, she was greatly surprised, for she thought that never before had she seen so fine a man. Long they talked, and then she was even more surprised, for when she came to know him, Nimue thought that she had never met such a man. From that day on they met together often, and as the days passed, Nimue came to love Pelleas more and more.

Finally, one day Nimue said to Pelleas, "Come, and love one who loves you."

Nimue and Pelleas were wed, and lived together long and happily, until both reached a ripe old age. Nimue helped King Arthur in all his wars, and after Arthur went away she helped the good kings of Britain who defended the folk after him, and Pelleas was ever a noble knight in the wars of the realm, and he alone survived all the wars unscathed to reach an advanced age, for Nimue took care that he should not be killed.

And when at last the time came for them to end their pilgrimage on this earth, Nimue and Pelleas died together, arm in arm, surrounded by their children, and their children's children, and the children of their grandchildren.

See *Le Morte D'Arthur*, by Sir Thomas Malory (circa 1450 A.D.)

Geo and Alette removed the roof of the Jeep to enjoy the morning sunshine as they drove. Coming down the ridge overlooking Portage Lake a fresh, cool breeze blew as they talked of Merlin and Arthur and Nimue.

"Nimue and Pelleas *are* names," Alette told him. "Nimue was trained by Merlin and eventually became The Lady of the Lake. Pelleas was her husband. He was a Knight of the Round Table."

"What does it mean," Geo asked, "that Nimue was The Lady of the Lake?"

"There was a lake in what today is called Glastonbury, in England, and in the lake was an island called Avalon," Alette explained. "The name Avalon means *The Isle of the Fruit of the Tree*."

"Like the image on the case," Geo said.

Alette nodded her head. "In Avalon was a college of learned sages," she continued, "masters of various disciplines, like medicine, astronomy, chemistry, mythology, history, and so on. The Lady of the Lake was the head of this college and she had charge of Caliburn."

"The shining sword," Geo said.

"Right," Alette said, "and that was the lake where Arthur got Caliburn."

"But I thought Merlin got Caliburn for Arthur?" Geo asked.

"Merlin helped Arthur get it," Alette confirmed, "but it wasn't actually Merlin's to give. He brought Arthur to the lake and helped Arthur get it, but it was The Lady of the Lake who gave it to him, though a different Lady than Nimue. Arthur received Caliburn from Nimue's predecessor before Nimue held that office, and Arthur was given Caliburn only on the condition that he return it to the lake again at the end of his life."

"Did he?" Geo asked.

"He did," Alette answered. "In his final battle, he slew Mordred, but Mordred gave Arthur a mortal wound. Knowing he was dying, Arthur asked to be taken to the lake. There he had Caliburn thrown into the water and then Nimue brought him in a boat to Avalon where she had some method of healing him, even when he was at the point of death."

"So she saved him?" Geo asked.

"Yes," Alette said, "and as he went off to Avalon he vowed that at Britain's hour of greatest need he would return again to help the people. That's why Arthur is *Rex Quondam Rexque Futurus, The King From Before Who Will Be King Once More*. But Arthur said that until that time came they would not see him anymore."

"So King Arthur is supposedly still alive?" Geo asked.

"And Merlin, too," Alette confirmed.

"But I thought Merlin went away?"

"He did," Alette said, "but no one knows where, or what he did after he left. He said he would remain hidden, working in secret, and continue to live and regenerate through the ages until the end of the world."

"What about Nimue and Pelleas?"

"They lived a long and happy life together," Alette said, "and died in each other's arms, surrounded by their family."

Geo reached over, took Alette's hand in his own,

and gave it a squeeze.

They continued talking as they drove, turning from paved roads to gravel, from gavel to dirt, and finally onto old, rutted logging tracks. When the Jeep could go no further they parked and began hiking up into the hills.

The trail they followed passed through a grove of pine trees. Fragrant pine needles crunched under their feet. Alette breathed deeply.

"Ahh," she sighed, "I love the smell of pine."

"Wait until you see the view," Geo said.

The trail narrowed and led finally to a rocky clearing on the crest of a hill. They walked out of the trees into the open and there was Lake Superior below them, sparkling in the sunlight.

"It's beautiful," Alette said.

"We'll rendezvous here," Geo said. "Get back here while you can still sustain The Light, before you have to let it go."

Alette nodded.

Geo opened the golden case, took out *The Book of Merlin*, and held it out to Alette.

"Are you ready?" he asked.

"Yes," Alette said and took the book.

In her hands the ink on the cover blurred and ran until the words reformed in French.

Alette took a deep breath and opened the book.

When it was opened power blasted out. The air sparkled with energy. It swirled around Alette and through its crackle Geo heard her reading aloud in French, "*Avant la lune ou le soleil . . .*"

When she completed the words of the *Cycle* the energy spun faster, forming into patterns that broke apart and coalesced again in new designs. The power rushed inward, converging on Alette and permeating into her.

As the energy coursed into her Alette dropped *The Book of Merlin* and it fell with its cover closed.

The last of the swirling power spiraled into Alette and for a moment all was still.

Suddenly, a great flash of Light burst from her.

Geo was blinded and felt his body freeze, rigid and immobile as The Light swept over him.

He heard Alette laugh. It was her same musical laugh he knew and loved, but with its beauty now amplified, as though the shining core of the laugh, the essence of what made it beautiful, had been distilled and purified and made greater, more intense, brighter and stronger.

Then he felt a rush of air and her laughter trailed away as Alette raced off through the forest.

The blast of Light pulsed outward and away from him. Geo's sight returned and his body was released. At the same instant birds flew up throughout the surrounding forest as everything sprang into a frenzy of noise and motion around him.

Alette was nowhere to be seen. *The Book of Merlin* lay on the ground where she had dropped it when the wash of power swept through her.

Geo reached down and picked it up.

Chapter 7

To the Sky

From Alette's research notes:

In the power of The Light they beheld one another and saw the great beauty of man.

See *The Post-Vulgate Quest for The Holy Grail*, by Anonymous (circa 1215 A.D.)

From Alette's research notes:

There is a secret known by some that allows them to ride the air so that they can be at London in the morning and Paris, or anywhere else the winds blow, in the afternoon.

See *The Life of Merlin*, by Geoffrey of Monmouth (circa 1150 A.D.)

From Alette's research notes:

Merlin went to Rome and wrote on the wall above the entrance to the Emperor's audience chamber in a language none there could read. For many years Merlin's writing remained where he had put it, for nothing they could do would wash it away or cover it over.

Then one day a man from a faraway land came, and the language of the writing was known to him. He read the writing aloud, and it said: "Know all men by this writing that the great stag with mighty antlers that came to the Emperor of Rome to give him warning was Merlin, in the form of a stag."

After the man had read these words, the letters disappeared, and nothing they could do would bring them back again.

See *The Story of Merlin*, by Anonymous (circa 1215 A.D.)

From Alette's research notes:

King Arthur stood with Merlin and his knights looking out on the vast camp of the enemy host. Thousands of tents and pavilions glittered in the sunlight and everywhere were seen their innumerable standards on tall poles.

King Arthur had only a small contingent of knights with him to fight so great a multitude.

"We have our work cut out for us," said King Arthur.

"Let me see if I can lessen it," said Merlin, and he began to weave his hands in the air and summoned a great wind and directed the wind so that it rushed into the enemy camp with such power that stakes were uprooted and tents flung into the sky and even men and horses were lifted from their feet and cast about in the great storm of wind. Thus were many of the enemy slain even before King Arthur or any of his knights fewtered a spear.

See *The Story of Merlin*, by Anonymous (circa 1215 A.D.)

Geo held the book and watched the ink on its cover dissolve into liquidity, swirl, and reform into English.

He opened the book and the surge of power erupted outward. But when he looked at the first page, he was surprised. Where he had read the words *The First Cycle* yesterday, the page was now blank. He turned to the next page and saw *The Second Cycle* written at its top. Instead of stopping to read *The Second Cycle*, Geo continued past it, turning pages to examine the rest of the book.

All the other pages were blank.

The book chooses what it allows to be read, Geo realized.

He turned back to *The Second Cycle*. Below the heading was written:

> *Having obtained the power of Light and discernment, you are ready to dance with the wind.*

Beneath this were the words of *The Second Cycle*. Geo read them aloud:

> *Into the air let me enter in*
> *To roam the sky and weave the wind*

The power whirled around him in flickering designs, then converged inward, penetrating into him and working through his body.

Suddenly a gust of wind enveloped him and Geo felt himself melt into it as if he had been sand or straw or dried leaves in autumn swirled away in a rush of air. He was carried up into the sky and an immense feeling of distance and speed filled him as the blast of wind roared around him and into him and through him.

Many times Geo had dreamed of flying, but this was different than any dream he'd ever had. It wasn't so much flying through the air, like a bird, as it was becoming wind, intermingling with it, being fused and interwoven into the flowing air.

He looked down at his body and saw it was ethereal, hazy and indistinct, a sparkle and brilliance in the air rather than solid matter, as if motion and energy and sunlight and sky had been poured into a mold of his body.

He clenched his hand into a fist and with the contraction of muscle and sinew felt the incredible power of the wind. He stretched out his arm, casting outward with the rushing sensation that coursed through him, and a mighty blast of wind thundered through the sky before him. He latched onto it and was swept high into the atmosphere.

Then he drew in with that same feeling of attenuation, of being knit into unison with the ever-vibrating air, and winds swirled toward him, gathering in as he pulled them close.

For a long time he rode through the heavens this way, flowing from one current of air into another, moving from channel to channel of the shifting winds. It was clear and cold and thundering and beautiful.

But the longer he mingled with the wind, the more its sharp chill pierced him and the more its constant, deafening roar began to crowd out his other senses. His sense of separation from it, the line of distinction between where it ended and he began, started to blur. He felt himself fraying, as if infinitesimal particles of himself were being swept away and lost in the ceaseless harrowing of the winds through him.

It was time to return again to the world of the earth.

He turned back toward the rendezvous point, scanning the forest below for Alette as he raced through the sky. He spotted her walking along a woodland path toward the clearing. She seemed exhausted, but excited, still overflowing with the experience of The

Light.

Geo swept down in a gusting swirl that spun around her, sending leaves and pine needles flying in the air.

Alette stopped and stared as he circled her in his shining, transparent form.

"Geo?" she asked.

He stepped out of the wind and materialized before her.

It startled him to have the omnipresent roaring of the wind suddenly cut off. The solidity of his limbs felt heavy and he shivered with cold.

"Geo!" Alette said. "It is you!"

She threw her arms around him and he felt her warmth flood into him.

"I saw you in the wind," she said, "it was like you were there, but you weren't."

"I was the wind," Geo said, "or I was in the wind, I'm not sure."

Alette looked up into his face.

"Geo," she said, "you should have seen yourself in The Light. The fire that burns in you, it's so beautiful."

They kissed.

Alette put her head on Geo's chest.

There was a rumble in the sky and they looked up to see a squadron of F-16's scream by overhead.

"The Light!" Alette said.

"After the reports yesterday," Geo said, "they were probably on alert. We better get back to the Jeep."

"Oh, I'm so hungry," Alette said.

"I know, The Light does that," Geo said, "and I'm

freezing. The wind, when you're immersed in it, chills you to the bone. Let's get home. I'll make dinner and start a fire. We've got a lot to talk about."

Pillar of Eliseg, located in Wales, United Kingdom, inscribed with a genealogy of kings, including Vortigern

Merlin and the Wildman

From Alette's research notes:

In the days of King Uther Pendragon enemies appeared off the coast of England in dragon-prowed ships so numerous they covered all the sea. King Uther was greatly alarmed and sent heralds in search of Merlin with instructions that they should find him and bring him to the King with all speed.

The heralds went out in every direction, scouring the realm for Merlin, for none knew where he was.

Some heralds went to the fastness of the Forest of Caledon, for it was rumored that Merlin walked that wilderness. The heralds entered the forest and within its precincts came to a clearing where they saw a huge Wildman who looked more like a thing of the forest than a person of human companionship. The Wildman was ugly, disheveled, and dirty, with a misshapen face. He had bushy eyebrows and a shaggy, unkempt beard. In his hands was a gigantic axe and he glowered at the heralds from across the clearing.

The heralds were exceedingly afraid and thought to flee, but the Wildman called to them: "I know why you are here, but you shall not find Merlin! If the King would speak with Merlin, the King must come himself to this forest!"

The heralds were astonished at the Wildman's speech and wondered how the Wildman could know their purpose.

"Where is Merlin?" they asked.

"Tell the King to come himself if he wishes to know, otherwise he shall not speak with Merlin," answered the Wildman.

The heralds tried various devices to learn from the Wildman the whereabouts of Merlin, but the Wildman would not answer them except to say that if the King wished to find Merlin, he must come himself to the forest and follow the Wildman.

When they saw they could get nowhere with the Wildman the heralds finally left and returned to the King and told him all about the matter.

The King desperately wanted to speak with Merlin, so he mounted his horse and told the heralds to lead on and they rode until they came to the Forest of Caledon. There the King followed the heralds into the forest and wondered how they were to find the Wildman.

But the Wildman found them.

The King saw the Wildman coming toward them in the forest and understood why the heralds had been afraid, for the Wildman was a giant fearsome to behold.

The Wildman said to the King: "So you wish to find Merlin, O King?"

"I do," answered the King. "Where is he?"

"Follow me and I will show you," answered the Wildman.

"Can you not tell me?" asked the King.

"If you wish to know, you must follow me, I will

say no more," answered the Wildman.

Then the King smiled, and began to laugh, for the King knew Merlin's ways, and knew that Merlin could take many forms of man or beast. For Merlin might appear now as a young man with downy cheek, now as an old man with hoary beard, now with one set of features, now with another, and even in the shape of animals of the wild. He could even take the form of strange creatures unknown in nature.

"Why do you laugh?" asked the Wildman.

"Why should I follow to find Merlin," answered the King, "when I speak to him now?"

Then the Wildman threw his head back and roared with laughter and before their eyes transformed into the shape of Merlin and the heralds were astounded.

Merlin said to the King, "Very astute of you, my King. Now come, for I have many things to show you and many things to tell you that you should know."

And the King and Merlin went off together beneath the shade of the trees.

See *Merlin*, by Robert de Boron (date unknown, believed circa 1190 A.D.); see *The Story of Merlin*, by Anonymous (circa 1215 A.D.)

Chapter 8

Plans and Preparations

From Alette's research notes:

Merlin told King Arthur, "I will help you obtain Caliburn, and do all that I can for you. I will give you what gifts I can, but know that there are things beyond my power and gifts that I cannot give."

See *The Merlin Continuation* of the Post-Vulgate Cycle, by Anonymous (circa 1235 A.D.); see *Le Morte D'Arthur*, by Sir Thomas Malory (circa 1450 A.D.)

Later that evening, after they had eaten, Geo and Alette sat together on the deck overlooking Portage Lake watching the lights of Houghton and Hancock shining on the water below.

"I don't think," Geo said, "that we should open *The Book of Merlin* anywhere around here again."

"The Light draws too much attention," Alette agreed.

"Yes," Geo said, "but it's more than that. Something about the power that comes from the book, it's . . ."

His voice trailed off as he tried to define the vague sense of foreboding that had taken hold of him since first opening the book.

"Like a beacon," Alette finished his sentence.

"That's it," Geo agreed. "And I'm not sure who or what it's calling. But I don't think we should keep opening it here."

"Then where?" asked Alette. "If we're going to learn more about it, we'll have to open it."

"I know," Geo said, "but it should be someplace far away. Far away from here, far away from other people, far away from everything."

They were silent as the sun sank lower in the sky.

Suddenly Alette said: "My father's cabin. It's perfect. It's on the other side of Superior and its out in the woods in the middle of nowhere."

Geo smiled. It was perfect, and he loved the cabin. It was a special place for both of them. That was where they really fell in love. Geo had met Alette when she first arrived in the Keweenaw on her sailboat, *The Morning Star*. It had been early in the morning at Copper Harbor. He was there painting when *The Morning Star* sailed in. Allette was coming to start her new job as a chemistry professor at Michigan Tech. She'd spent the summer sailing Superior and was tanned deep brown with her strawberry blond hair bleached gold by the sun.

Geo watched her bring in *The Morning Star* smart and lively, deft and nimble as she moved about the boat securing lines and reefing sails.

A low fog hung just above Superior's surface that

morning, as it often does, and in the slanting rays of the sun the mist glowed golden. A chilly breeze blew and waves beat on the shore.

"Can I lend a hand?" Geo called.

"*Merci!*" Alette called back. "Can you fasten a line?"

"Sure!" Geo said, putting down his brushes and palette and stepping from his easel.

She threw him a line that he caught it in the air and made fast to the pier.

He helped her get *The Morning Star* secured then took her to breakfast. That was the beginning of a magical year. Geo took Alette on adventures all over Copper Country, sharing with her his favorite places. Alette loved the outdoors as much as he did. Through the remainder of the summer and into the autumn they hiked, swam, kayaked, and camped. When the heavy snows of winter in the Upper Peninsula came they snowshoed, skated, went cross country skiing, and downhill skiing and snowboarding at Mont Ripley.

Alette in turn shared with Geo her knowledge of bushcraft gleaned from years in the Canadian wilderness with her trapper father, and introduced him to traditional folk music and a whole new world of poetry. She went with him on his painting excursions, bringing a picnic basket and her guitar. She would recite poetry and play and sing while Geo worked at his easel.

He loved listening to her. Her voice was gorgeous, just like she was, and she was a gifted musician. When Geo took a break from painting they would sit together, eating and talking. And when Geo's painting for the day was done they would lay on their backs on the blanket, holding hands, watching the clouds float by overhead, and kiss, and talk, and enjoy being together.

At the end of Michigan Tech's academic year Alette invited Geo to meet her father and stay with them for a few weeks at her father's cabin. They sailed across Superior together on *The Morning Star* to a bay where a trail led inland to the cabin. Alette's father, Théodore, was an old hunter and trapper, quiet and tough and strong. He was used to spending time alone in the wilderness, as was Geo, though Geo's time in the backcountry was spent with paint and canvas rather than trap and rifle. The two understood and liked each other right from the start.

It was a glorious summer, hiking and painting, helping Théodore in the bush, and spending nights around the campfire under the stars. Some days Alette took Geo cruising on *The Morning Star* to explore the coast or one of Superior's many islands. They would pick a place on the charts and sail to it, anchor, and take the dingy ashore. There they'd walk beaches searching for agates—the semi-precious stones of brilliant hues polished smooth and lustrous by the sand and waves of Superior—or explore inland, climbing rocks and tramping forests. They picked wild blueberries and strawberries and ate them with their picnic lunches in unbelievably beautiful spots atop cliffs above Superior's shining waters.

And nights around the campfire at the cabin were amazing. So far out in the wilderness away from everything the wonders of the heavens were revealed in the Milky Way spread above them, ablaze with millions of twinkling stars. Sometimes they talked, sometimes Geo and Théodore sang along with Alette while she played guitar, sometimes Alette and Théodore took turns reciting poetry from memory. And sometimes they all sat together in easy, companionable silence, listening to the crackle of the fire and watching red sparks rise into the night.

Geo treasured the opportunity of that summer to experience Alette's life at the cabin. He got to see her in her old home place that she loved so much with the father she loved so much, and through that came to know her and love her even more deeply.

It also helped him appreciate in a new way her stories of growing up with her father in the wilderness. Her mother, Margaret, died when Alette was four. Alette was named for her, her full name was Margaret Alette Martel. Her parents called her by her middle name to distinguish mother from daughter. After her mother's death, her father raised Alette on his own. Alette's only remaining memories of her mother were images and impressions, but they were full of love and warmth, song and laughter, and they were precious to her.

When Alette was growing-up she and her father lived in a house in town during the school year so Alette could attend school. Early on she showed extraordinary intellectual ability and her father encouraged her academic career all the way to her Ph.D. in chemistry and her eventual appointment as a professor at Michigan Tech.

But whenever school was out, father and daughter were back at the cabin in the woods, camping and hiking, hunting and running trap lines, and singing around campfires under starry skies where Théodore recited poems until Alette learned them all by heart.

Geo was also glad for the summer the three of them spent together at the cabin because, though none of them knew it at the time, it was the only chance Geo would ever have to be with both Alette and her father together at the cabin. Théodore died the following year during Alette's second year at Michigan Tech.

He had not been feeling well, so he closed up the cabin and headed to town to see a doctor. From that first doctor's appointment he was sent immediately to hospital. He checked into the hospital that afternoon and never left. Within a few weeks he was gone. Alette and Geo went to him right away as soon as they received word and they were with him at the end. That, too, had been a blessing, one for which they were both grateful.

After the funeral they stopped briefly at the cabin to see that all was in order and buttoned-up for winter. It had been almost a year ago now that they'd locked the cabin door and returned to Hancock.

The cabin wouldn't be the same without Théodore, but this would give Alette a chance to be back, to sort through things and memories, and begin thinking about what to do with the cabin and her father's possessions.

And Alette was right. The cabin was remote and isolated, the perfect place to investigate *The Book of*

Merlin.

"Brilliant," Geo agreed.

"*The Morning Star* is ready," Alette said. They had already been sailing this season and Alette had been preparing to return to the cabin at some point in the summer. "We can get some supplies on board and leave tomorrow."

"Let's make a list of what we'll need," Geo said, "but let's do it inside. I'm freezing. I think I'm still cold from the wind."

They went in and Geo built a fire. Tonight it was Alette's turn to lay down on the couch. She stretched out, exhausted from The Light, and sighed deeply as she closed her eyes.

Geo got a pad of paper and a pen and began writing a list of the things they'd need. After a few minutes he read the list aloud and asked, "What else can you think of?"

Alette didn't answer.

Geo looked over the top of the pad.

Alette was fast asleep.

He smiled and set his list aside. He stood and went to get a blanket. He brought it back, covered her, unlaced her boots and gently pulled them from her feet. Without waking, Alette gave a contented murmur, turned onto her side and pulled the blanket up to her chin.

Geo went back to the chair and in the flickering light of the fire finished making plans for the journey.

Chapter 9

They Come

From Alette's research notes:

Fafnir was born a man but became a dragon, murdering men and consuming them, spewing his poisonous breath before him always, and putting terror into the hearts of men the better to slay them.

See *The Saga of the Volsungs*, by Anonymous (circa 1250 A.D.)

From Alette's research notes:

Then the cruel invader came with their dragons, slaying the people, burning and destroying all things.

See *The Alliterative Morte Arthure*, by Anonymous (circa 1360 A.D.)

Geo stood on the dock in the early morning light. It

was chilly beside the water. He wore a t-shirt with a flannel shirt over it. The golden case slung on a leather strap that hung from his shoulder across his chest. They'd found places to attach a strap to the case and Alette fastened one of her guitar straps to it. *The Book of Merlin* was inside the case. Geo could feel a faint tingle from it through his shirt.

The Morning Star was ready to sail. Food and clothes were stowed, along with a massive stack of books Alette had checked out from the university library about Merlin and Arthur and Caliburn. In true Alette fashion she had started a research journal to record her findings related to *The Book of Merlin*. It too was aboard. All was ready.

Now Geo waited for Alette to return from a final run to town for a last few odds and ends.

He looked across Lake Superior. Sunlight sparkled on the endlessly moving water. The wind was cool against his face. He felt a yearning to enter again into its rush and soar high above the great inland sea that lay before him.

Soon, he thought. *When we get to the cabin.*

Suddenly his thoughts were shattered by a blast of Light that erupted from town behind him. Geo was frozen, held immobile and blinded as The Light washed over him.

Then The Light pulsed onward, his vision returned, and his body was released. He turned and saw a white flash streaking toward him from town, coming across the Bridge. Onrushing wind buffeted him and then Alette was there, standing in front of him, glowing with

The Light.

She let The Light extinguish and threw her arms around him.

"Geo!" she cried. "They're here! They're here . . . and . . . and . . ." her voice broke and she sobbed. "They're more horrible than you can imagine!" she cried.

"Who?" Geo asked, startled, he had never seen her like this. "What happened?"

An eerie, shrieking howl rose from town. First one weird voice, then others joined it in a repellent cacophony that sent chills down Geo's spine. But something in that mad shrieking also kindled anger within him, instantly stirring his blood for battle, as if some ancient instinct, long dormant and forgotten but always laying just beneath the surface, had suddenly been triggered.

"Get onboard *The Morning Star*," Geo told her. "I want you out of here."

"It's the Spartoi!" Alette cried, "The dragon-men! They're here and . . ."

She broke down again.

Geo held her. "It's okay," he said. "Tell me what happened."

"They *smelled* me!" Alette cried. "They were like a pack of animals, and the sounds they made . . . they kept shouting at me to give them Nimue's Gift . . . they tried to take me . . . they grabbed me . . ."

Geo's eyes flashed. The rage already kindled inside him erupted into an inferno.

"I tried to break free," Alette continued, "but they

73

held me and wouldn't let me go and they laughed and . . ."

Geo's jaw muscles clenched. They had laid hands on Alette. He would smash them. Whoever they were, he would make sure they never dared do such a thing again.

"Then The Light burst within me," Alette went on, "and I ran . . ."

Alette started crying again.

"Where are they?" Geo asked, his voice low and intense, bristling with rage.

Tears streamed down Alette's face and she drew a long, ragged breath. She pointed back toward town, then hugged Geo tight again.

"I didn't know what to do," she said, "and The Light, when it came, what I saw in them . . . it was horrible . . . so horrible . . . there's something in them that's . . . it's so dark . . . it's not human!"

"Get on *The Morning Star*," Geo ordered.

She raised her head to look at him and what he saw in her eyes, the fear and desperation, things she should never have had to know, made him shake with fury.

The howling started again, drawing nearer.

"Get on board," Geo said. "Start the engine and I'll push you off."

"What about you?" she asked. "You have to come. Don't leave me alone."

"I won't leave you alone," he promised. "I'll come to you. But if I come on board now they'll follow. I'm going to make sure they don't. Hurry. I'll push you off. Get through the channel and keep going. I'm going to stop them on the Bridge. After that I'll come to you. You just keep going. Get to the cabin. I'll ride the wind to *The Morning Star* or else meet you at the cabin. Wait for me there."

"Geo, you can't," she pleaded, "don't leave me alone!"

"I'll come to you, I promise," he said.

The howling grew louder, approaching fast.

"No more time to talk!" Geo said.

Alette went on board *The Morning Star* and Geo cast off lines.

Alette started the engines.

Geo let the power of The Light begin to burn within him. He watched his hands and arms glow brighter and brighter. When he felt the strength of The Light coursing through him, he pushed *The Morning Star* out, turning its prow in the direction of the channel leading to the Keweenaw Bay, and gave a great heave to send it surging on its way with a spray of foam thrown up from its bows.

Geo let The Light drain from him as he watched *The Morning Star* make way.

Two channels led out from Portage Lake. One was at the eastern end of the lake and led to Superior at Keweenaw Bay, on the east side of the Keweenaw Peninsula. The other channel was at the opposite side of the lake, at its western end, and led out to Superior on the western side of the Keweenaw Peninsula, on its western shore that faced toward Isle Royale.

Alette was heading to the eastern channel and Keweenaw Bay. It was in that direction, far across

Superior's icy waves on the other side of the great lake, that her father's cabin lay.

"I love you!" Geo shouted.

"I love you!" Alette yelled back.

"Remember!" she shouted. "You promised!"

The torn sound of her voice cut Geo to the heart.

"I remember!" Geo called back.

The howling behind him rose in pitch. Geo turned and saw them: six men loping along the Bridge, loose limbed and shambling, moving like wild things, sniffing the air as they went, as if following a trail by scent.

The sight of them set Geo's teeth on edge. There was something utterly vile about them. He ran up onto the Bridge and started across it toward them.

They saw him coming, sniffed the air, and broke out in cackling and started an insane capering.

Geo ran straight at them.

The six men spread out in a line and charged at him.

Geo knotted his hands into fists and felt the golden case slap against his side as he sprinted forward. It flashed, glinting in the sunlight.

"Nimue's Gift!" one of them yelled, pointing.

They started their mad howling again with a new intensity and raced at Geo eagerly, wildly.

Geo's skin crawled. He clenched his jaw. His only thought was that they had put their hands on Alette. They would learn to never do that again.

Geo targeted the man nearest him in the oncoming line, lowered his shoulder, and barreled straight into him.

The impact as Geo smashed into him crushed the man to the ground, but immediately another of them ran at Geo from the side.

Geo whirled and swung his fist.

The blow hammered into the man's chin, snapping his head back and dropping him in a heap to the pavement.

Someone slammed into Geo's blind side. Geo staggered, but stayed up. The man held Geo, pinning one of Geo's arms against his side, and tried to pull him down. Geo twisted toward his assailant and raised his free hand in a fist to strike. The man bared his teeth and bit savagely into Geo's arm that he held pinned against Geo's side. Geo felt the man's teeth fasten onto his flesh. Geo drove his fist into the man's head, pounding again and again until he, too, went down.

The man rolled over, scrambled out of Geo's reach, and screamed, "He does not bleed! He does not bleed!"

The other two Geo had knocked down were back on their feet now also. Geo was hit from behind. Strong arms locked around him. Someone else smashed into his side, and then another. They piled onto him. Hands grabbed and pulled at him, he was punched and kicked. They beat him and tried to pull him to the ground.

"It is mine Kaya!" yelled one of the Spartoi.

"Never Gibber! I will eat you first!" Kaya shouted back.

The Spartoi struggled against each other even as they gripped Geo and pressed down on him like a dark wave.

Geo stumbled. He swayed under their weight and

felt himself falling.

The Spartoi roared in mad eagerness as Geo's legs buckled.

Then The Light burst from Geo in a great blast. Its power filled him and he shook the Spartoi off, sending them flying as he flung them from his back and arms. He ran at the nearest and lashed out with a burning fist. He struck the Spartoi in the gut and the man was thrown backwards through the air to sprawl on the ground, unconscious.

Then Geo stopped in shock.

He saw what Alette had described to him. The vision of The Light revealed within the Spartoi not a bright flame, but something dark and writhing.

It was horrifying.

The blast of Light pulsed past and the Spartoi were released from its hold. But freed from The Light they did not attack Geo. Instead, they rushed on the Spartoi Geo had knocked out with his burning fist, pouncing on him and . . .

Geo turned away.

He wanted to wretch.

It was too gruesome to watch. The other five Spartoi *consumed* the man where he lay on the concrete.

With the perception of The Light Geo saw the writhing darkness inside the attacking Spartoi rip and tear at the downed Spartoi like spectral serpents, devouring the man, absorbing him within themselves. It was something physical, but more than physical.

Geo reeled. The world had gone insane. His only

thought was that they must be destroyed.

He whirled and charged into them, slamming a fist into the ribs of one of the Spartoi where he hunched over the remains of the fallen man. Geo's blow sent the Spartoi spiraling through the air. Again, the others pounced on their stricken comrade. The biggest of the four remaining Spartoi snarled and slashed at the other three, driving them back. He fell on the stricken Spartoi and ripped into his body.

"Gibber! We want dust!" one of the others yelled, but the big one called Gibber growled and pulled the body closer.

Geo charged again and the dragon-men darted away, their twisting, spectral serpents writhing within them.

Gibber dragged the remnant of the carcass with him as he fled, continuing to feed even as he ran. Geo stared. He could actually see Gibber growing larger before his eyes as Gibber consumed and absorbed the fallen Spartoi.

Gibber pointed at Geo and screeched, "Burn him out! Kaya! Madne! Krule! Make him burn until The Light is gone and then we shall all feast!"

Geo was stunned at the words.

They know, he realized. *They know about The Light.*

The Spartoi circled around him, leering, waiting, biding their time. One would feint a strike, then dash back when Geo turned to face him, while they all continued circling beyond his reach.

They're burning me out, Geo thought. *They know I*

can't keep The Light long and they're waiting until I have to let it go.

Already it was ebbing as his body struggled to sustain its power.

And they know it, Geo thought.

"He fades!" cackled Gibber. "Nimue's Gift will be mine!"

"Ours!" one screamed back.

"Mine, Kaya!" shouted Gibber. "And I'll take your dust with it if you cross me!"

Geo looked out over the Bridge and across the water. *The Morning Star* was making way but was still in Portage Lake. He had to give Alette more time.

He turned and sprinted toward the other side of the Bridge, the side facing west, away from Alette. The Spartoi scattered out of his path.

Geo didn't chase them. He kept on full tilt toward the edge of the Bridge.

"He fears!" yelled Gibber. "He is ours!"

Geo knew the eyes of the Spartoi were on him, not Alette, and that was what he wanted. If he fought them here, now, and fell, they would have him and Alette both. He had to be sure she was safe. He had to give her time to get away. And he could not sustain The Light much longer.

"He fears! He fears!" Kaya and the other Spartoi took up Gibber's call.

Geo ignored them and ran on. He sprang to the Bridge railing and launched himself off the Bridge into the sky, far out over the lake.

He let The Light go out of him as he hurtled

through the air and felt an immediate relief as its burning ceased and the cold air washed over him.

Behind him on the Bridge the dragon-men howled.

Geo transformed into the ethereal form of sky and wind and swept into a swift current of air rushing up from the surface of the water. Riding the updraft he turned to look back at the Spartoi.

What he saw shook him.

Dragon bones from the dragon slain by Saint Donato are displayed behind the altar of The Church of Santa Maria and San Donato in Murano, Italy

Chapter 10

Dragons in the Sky

From Alette's research notes:

Dragons appeared in the skies over England, flying on great wings and spewing fire from their mouths. The people saw them in the sky and wondered what it could mean. Then there came the dragon-men in their dragon-prowed ships with sword and fire to kill and destroy the people.

See *The Anglo-Saxon Chronicle* (793 A.D.)

From Alette's research notes:

The dragon-man Fafnir possessed the helmet of terror, which put fear into the hearts of men, and Fafnir used it to slay many. When Sigurd slew Fafnir the helmet came into his possession, along with many another ancient and curious treasure from Fafnir's hoard.

See *The Poetic Edda* (circa 900 A.D.)

Gibber pointed at Geo where he weaved through the air and shouted, "I see you! You cannot hide! Run if you will, but I shall catch you!"

Gibber sprinted toward the Bridge railing, jumped onto it, and leapt out over the water as Geo had done. Then something hideous began. As Geo stared, Gibber changed mid-air in a terrible transformation. His neck elongated and great wings unfurled from his back, opening like dark sails to catch the wind. A tail emerged behind him, sinuous and powerful. All the dimensions of his body expanded and he grew to enormous size. His hands twisted into claws with long, dark talons. His head mutated into the great, heavy head of a dragon. Jagged teeth showed as he leered at Geo.

The dragon's huge batwings beat the air and it climbed into the sky, shaking its head and roaring with laughter as Geo gaped. Smoke trailed from its nostrils.

"Merlin didn't tell you about *me*, did he, little sparrow?" Gibber taunted. "He didn't tell you I would be like *this! Strong!* Why do you think he sent *you* to face us instead of coming *himself*? Did you ever wonder at that? Why do you think he gave you the paltry things he calls *gifts?* The few meager tricks his stingy, clinging heart is willing to share? What did you think was in it for him? Or didn't you have the presence of mind to ask that? Think on it now! Ask yourself what calculation lay behind his gifts! Wonder at that, little sparrow!"

Geo hesitated a moment, trying to take in what he was seeing. The dragon was huge, the size of a bus, covered in black scales, with shining red eyes and enormous wings fanning the air like a hurricane.

Then Geo turned and sped away on the wind.

"Fly away if you can little sparrow!" the dragon bellowed after him. "But can you fly through *fire?*"

The dragon cackled with wicked laughter, opened its mouth, and spewed a thundering jet of flame straight at Geo.

Looking back over his shoulder Geo saw the blast coming and wheeled into a spiral of wind that veered off at a sharp angle, carrying him out of the fire's path.

The spout of flame sizzled past, missing Geo, but the shock of its force knocked him from the current of wind that he rode. Geo fell, but reached out his hands and summoned a new wind that came shooting up off the lake to bear him away.

Geo turned the direction of the wind to swing out at a sharp angle away from the line of the dragon's flight.

The dragon laughed and banked into a wide turn on its great wings to follow after him.

Geo watched the dragon's ponderous arc through the sky. It was big, powerful, and fast, but it could not match the nimbleness of Geo's aerial maneuvers, the sharpness of his turns and his sudden sheering off in new directions when he shifted from one stream of wind to another.

Then Geo saw the other three Spartoi coming up behind Gibber, each transformed into a dragon and beating their wings in furious pursuit.

And there, further out, beyond the dragons, beyond the Bridge, near the end of Portage Lake and the entrance to the channel leading out to Keweenaw Bay, Geo saw *The Morning Star.*

Alette's escape was all that mattered.

Geo slowed, allowing the dragons to close on him. When the dragons saw themselves gaining on their prey they bellowed in eagerness and strove all the harder to reach him.

Geo let them narrow the gap further, whetting their desire.

They were focused only on him while unseen behind them *The Morning Star* entered the channel.

The dragons came on faster and faster.

Geo continued to check his speed, going slowly so that he stayed just ahead of them, leading them over Portage Lake and past it to the west, flying above the forests of the Keweenaw Peninsula toward its western coast. He reached Lake Superior's shoreline, crossed its threshold, and was out over open water. He looked back again for *The Morning Star*. He could no longer see it. It was hidden from view somewhere far behind him, beyond the stone ridges and tall pine forests of the Keweenaw.

Alette was away.

A jet of fire rushed toward him and the dragons roared as they hurtled through the air after him.

Geo turned and wheeled into a new, fast-moving stream of wind that rushed him away to the west, across the water in the opposite direction from where Alette sailed *The Morning Star*.

The powerful new wind he rode sped Geo far out in front of the pursuing dragons and they screamed in rage behind him.

Chapter 11

The Hidden Places

From Alette's research notes:

We paddled our canoes past a cliff and saw a strange sight. High on the face of the cliff was a huge painting of a dragon, terrible to behold.

See *The Journal of Father Jacques Marquette* (1673 A.D.)

From Alette's research notes:

There was a legend told by the people of that land concerning the great painting of the dragon on the cliff. It was said that long ago the dragon had come across the salt sea in search of human flesh to eat, for they say that it hungered always to consume men, and it devoured the people constantly wherever it could find them. Until, at last, a great chief appeared among the people to fight the dragon. The chief sacrificed himself at a tree in battle with the dragon, and though the chief was terribly stricken, even unto death, the great chief defeated the dragon and it was utterly destroyed. Then, they say, the great chief arose again

*and was not dead, but lived, and the people painted
the dragon on the cliff that all generations might
remember the victory over the dread beast.*

See *The Legend of the Piasa of Alton, Illinois*

Geo rode one channel of wind after another,
shifting from gust to gust, darting back and forth across
the sky, always heading north and west across *Gitche
Gumee*, the Big Sea Water. He was leading the dragons
away from the course that Alette sailed somewhere far
behind him.

He had slowed again to allow the dragons to draw
near. All four dragons cleaved through the sky after him
in their bulky, powerful flight, taunting him as they
pursued.

"Feel how the sky chills!" Kaya yelled. "Feel how
the wind chaffs! What will you do when you can no
longer fly, little sparrow? We do not tire! Come, give us
Nimue's Gift!"

"You belong to the Sixth Day, little sparrow, we are
sons of the First!" shouted Gibber. "How can you stand
against us!"

Geo continued crisscrossing the sky in his erratic
flight, staying just beyond the dragons' reach. He
wanted to tantalize them and keep them eager in their
pursuit to draw them farther from Alette. So he would
let them close on him, then cut through the sky at a

sharp angle to dart away, spinning through the air like an autumn leaf dancing on the breeze while they swung in their wide, sweeping turns after him.

But the dragons are right, Geo thought, *I can't keep this up.*

The cold bit into him fiercely and he was tiring.

He could no longer see the Keweenaw Peninsula behind him. Ahead, blue and hazy in the distance, the great bluffs and headlands of the northwest coast were coming into view. Somewhere there, amid those towering rocks, with their deep clefts and broken crags, he could find a place to hide and rest to recover his strength.

He remembered the legends of the *Maymaygwayshi*, the Rock Wizards. They were said to have lived in caves hidden in the sheer cliff faces of the towering islands and remote coastlines of The Big Sea Water, and atop the plateaus crowning the stony islands that jutted like pillars from the cold waters of Lake Superior. Legend said it was the Rock Wizards who made the mysterious images of battles and dragons and horned dragon-men that were painted on cliffs hundreds of feet above the water's surface all around Superior.

In the 1820's, Henry Schoolcraft, a writer and explorer from New York, came to the wild waters of North America's inland seas. He married an Indian princess and lived with her on an island in the Great Lakes. It was he who wrote of the rock paintings. An old Indian had given Schoolcraft a birchbark scroll with a map showing the hidden places of the Rock Wizards' images. Later scholars dismissed Schoolcraft's accounts until, in the 1950's, a man outfitted a ship and followed the directions left by Schoolcraft and found the spectacular pictograph site of Agawa just where Schoolcraft said it would be.

Other sites described by Schoolcraft still remained to be rediscovered, awaiting future expeditions to follow the directions from the ancient birchbark scroll.

Other early explorers had also noted pictographs. When Father Marquette paddled down the Kankakee River he encountered a huge painting of a dragon on a high cliff. It depicted the dragon slain by the great chief Ouatogo, who legend says sacrificed himself at a tree set high on a rocky cliff overlooking the water in order to defeat a terrible dragon that was devouring his people. The dragon had come across the salt sea to feed on human flesh. After the battle, the victorious Ouatago, though it had appeared he was mortally wounded, was restored to life.

Geo flew on, the cold winds above Lake Superior piercing through him. The Light had already taken a toll earlier and now he had been too long harrowed in the wind. He was bone weary.

Fire sizzled at his heels as once again the dragons closed on him.

"Merlin didn't tell you about our fire, did he?" shrieked Madne. "What else did he keep from you?"

Geo swung into a new current of air. It was time to leave them behind. He needed a hiding place, somewhere he could return to his own form and rest. He was so cold it hurt.

The cliffs. He had to reach the cliffs.

"Run if you can little sparrow!" Gibber laughed behind him. "But when you can no longer ride the wind you will fall like a stone and we will be there to pounce!"

Hammer of Thor, located in Quebec, Canada; a prehistoric megalithic monument believed to have been erected by Norsemen

Chapter 12

Whispers on the Wind

From Alette's research notes:

Sometimes the sky-roamers can be seen as they fly, weaving in and out of the wind. But they must beware, for if they stay too long in the wind they may not be able to return again to their bodies of dust and clay.

See *The Poetic Edda* (circa 900 A.D.)

From Alette's research notes:

Merlin loved music. When he was weary and troubled in mind or body or spirit, he turned to music to be restored. He was skilled himself with both instrument and voice and sometimes went about under the guise of a minstrel.

See *The Life of Merlin,* by Geoffrey of Monmouth (circa 1150 A.D.); *The Story of Merlin,* by Anonymous (circa 1215 A.D.)

Alette is away, Geo thought. *Now I have to find a place to hide.*

He needed to warm himself and recover his strength.

Summoning winds from where they thundered fast across Lake Superior, he wove them together in a great torrent that shook the water like a typhoon. The dragons reeled in its wash.

Geo threw his out his arms to send the storming blast rocketing toward the dark headlands to the northwest and dove into its midst. Instantly he was swept away as the tempest roared over the crashing waves of Lake Superior.

The powerful, twisting winds cut into him like sword thrusts, rending his vaporous form.

He gasped and struggled to hold himself together, afraid the hurricane blast would scatter him like dust. He wondered what would happen if he were torn apart, ripped to bits and flung to the four winds, unable to reform again. Maybe that was why in high, lonely places whispers sometimes seemed to mingle in the wind just beyond the edge of hearing.

Behind him the dragons screamed in rage as they watched their prey suddenly streak away from them across the thrashing sea.

Geo had to ride this wind, stay in it, bear the pain of its cold, and hold himself together amid its winnowing. He had to endure it as long as he could to reach the cliffs and find a place to hide.

He flew on, numb from the cold, his senses overpowered by the thundering of the wind.

He was dimly aware of Isle Royale flashing by below. The largest island in Lake Superior, it stretches forty-five miles long and nine wide. Geo heard its dark pines creak along the cliff tops as he tore through the sky above them.

The outlines of The Sleeping Giant loomed before him. A mass of rock rising twelve hundred feet above Lake Superior in a sheer, vertical wall of stone, it was topped by a long, narrow plateau that formed an island in the sky.

Lake Superior had hundreds of such isolated realms, unknown and unexplored, hidden atop the cliff palisades of its rocky islands and coastline. Their unique combinations of altitude and latitude, of soil and moisture, created miniature ecosystems where rare orchids bloomed and exotic species throve. Some held other secrets, like the small island just a few hundred yards from shore where the largest silver deposit in the world was discovered, reaching deep into the earth far below the lake's bed.

Unexplained magnetic anomalies hid other islands from navigational electronics and sent ships veering off course. On some islands and along remote stretches of coastline the remains of ancient stone forts still stood, built by vanished peoples whose civilizations had long ago disappeared.

Somewhere among that maze of islands and inlets, bays and fjords, Geo would find his hiding place.

He looked back. The dragons were visible now only as dark specks flying above the surface of the water.

A bloom of fire sprouted from one, reflecting red-orange in the waves of Lake Superior below.

The dragons were far behind him, but they still followed, and they burned with rage.

Cliffs along the shore of Lake Superior

Chapter 13

The Cave of the Rock Wizards

From Alette's research notes:

Merlin was a seeker of treasures and a finder of treasures, whether buried in the earth or sunken below rolling waves.

And Merlin was a sharer of treasures. He brought King Arthur to a place in the weald and said to him: "Dig here, and you will find a great hoard of gold and silver from ages past. Use it to equip your army that you may defeat the dragon-men."

King Arthur dug where Merlin directed and found a vast treasure. With it he armed knights and gathered a host for war.

See *The Story of Merlin*, by Anonymous (circa 1215 A.D.); see *Le Morte D'Arthur*, by Sir Thomas Malory (circa 1450 A.D.)

With Isle Royale behind him, Geo veered up the coast past The Sleeping Giant to Black Bay Peninsula and the hundreds of nameless islands scattered from

Thunder Bay to the Slates, a group of islands in the far north of Lake Superior.

He searched the towering stone faces of cliffs and islands as the wind carried him through channels and rocky fjords. Finally he found what he was seeking: a dark opening of deep shadow in a sunlit wall of stone on an island that rose with sheer sides from the cold waters of Superior. Geo directed the wind toward it. When he reached the island he drifted downward along the face of the cliff. Falling past the opening he caught a glimpse of a shadowed interior. It was a cave.

He spiraled back upward on a rising draft of warmer air until he hovered before the opening. Sunlight illuminated a patch of stone floor at the cave entrance. Geo stepped out of the wind into the sunlight, materializing back into his own body. The stone of the cave's doorstep glowed with the sun's absorbed heat and it flowed into him. Geo lay down in the golden light, warmth radiating into his stiff, cold limbs from the stone floor and the rays of beaming sunshine. He closed his eyes. For a long time he lay still, feeling the sun on his skin and the rising and falling of his chest as he breathed. Sensations of red light and warmth and the rhythm of his breathing filled his wind-numbed mind. Exhausted, he drifted off to sleep.

* * *

Geo woke with a shiver. The sun had moved in the sky and he now lay in shadow. Wind off the water whistled in through the cave entrance and chilled him.

He looked out and saw the long shadow cast by the island upon the dark, restless waters of Lake Superior. Across the far horizon clouds were crimson with the red light of the waning of the day.

Gazing out, Geo saw no sign of the dragons.

Where are they? he wondered.

He sat-up and rubbed his arms and legs to put some warmth into them. He stood and moved farther into the cave, away from the cold wind blowing in through its entrance. In the shadowy dark his foot kicked something. He looked down. In the gloom he saw clay pots lined along the cave wall. He bent to examine them, and then he saw lines painted on the cave wall behind them. He stepped back to see the whole wall.

In the fading light he could just make it out.

It was a painting of a dragon.

And not just a dragon, a battle. A band of warriors were attacking the dragon. Arrows and spears flew through the air at the beast and one feathered shaft lodged in the dragon's breast. A warrior held his bow aloft in triumph at having dealt the fatal blow.

What struck Geo was the accuracy of the dragon's depiction. It was so true to the dragons that pursued him, he knew that whoever made this painting had seen dragons.

And they painted this, Geo thought, *to show that the dragons exist.*

But he knew that wasn't right.

No, Geo suddenly understood, *not to show that dragons exist, to show that dragons can be slain.*

The painting wasn't made to memorialize the dragon. It was made to memorialize the victory.

Geo touched the golden case containing *The Book of Merlin* that hung at his side. Power tingled into his fingertips. Nimue's Gift.

That was what the dragons wanted. And they knew he had it. They had seen it and it was for this that they pursued him.

Merlin said that when the book was opened they would feel the release of its power and come. And they had.

Merlin also said that it could be used to defeat the dragons.

Geo went back to the cave entrance and looked out.

Where are they? he wondered. *Where is Alette? And what will we do when I reach her?*

Could they evade the dragons indefinitely, living forever on the run? Even if they could, what kind of life would that be?

Geo shook his head. He didn't know what he and Alette would do, but he didn't have to know right now. What he had to do now was draw the dragons to himself again. He must lead the chase anew and keep them from Alette. He had to give her time to reach her father's cabin.

Then, when he had led the dragons to someplace far away, he would slip away from them unseen and dash to Alette on the wind faster than the dragons could follow.

He would keep his promise.

After that, he and Alette could figure out their next

move together.

Geo went back to the cave entrance. He didn't know how long he had slept, but the sky was deepening to purple in the advancing dusk. It was time.

He took *The Book of Merlin* from its golden case and opened it. Power welled up from the book and burst into the gathering night.

Like a signal flare, Geo thought.

He turned past blank pages until he came to *The Third Cycle*.

Suddenly his eyes flicked upward. Something, some motion, had drawn his attention.

Then he saw them.

Black shapes against the sky, coming over the water. A red spark flared from one of them.

Dragons.

Geo smiled. It seemed they could be counted on to come when called. They wanted Nimue's Gift badly and they would race to reach it.

The dragons seemed to know all about The Light and the ethereal transformation into wind and all about Merlin. Now here was something he knew about them. It was a start.

But then he realized he knew something else about them. He thought of the cave painting behind him.

He knew the dragons could be slain.

Chapter 14

Into the Deep

From Alette's research notes:

I saw him in the water near Pie Island. He was a man, or in the shape of a man, but he was made of water. He was in the water, but made of water, shining water. He looked up at me from the water and I saw his eyes, luminescent, looking at me.

See *Lake Superior*, by Grace Lee Nute regarding the sworn testimony of Venant St. Germain relating his encounter with a merman at Pie Island in Lake Superior on May 3, 1782 A.D.

Geo stood at the entrance to the cave high in the cliff above the crashing waves of Superior, and spoke aloud the words of *The Third Cycle* from *The Book of Merlin*:

Where are gathered the heavens below
Let me enter within the water's flow

Power cascaded and swirled around him, coalescing thicker as it spun faster and faster, enveloping him until all the world outside the blaze of energy became muted and hazy beyond the bright veiling of power.

The whirling energy spiraled inward and penetrated into him, moving through him, rippling through muscle and throbbing in his bones.

Suddenly it was over, and Geo's perception of the world was different. He was aware of moisture in the air around him, in the clouds above, and, overpowering all else, was the vastness of Lake Superior below. He longed to join it, to enter into it.

Another jet of flame flashed over the water.

The dragons were coming.

Geo looked down and saw his body was no longer flesh but had become something flowing and translucent, shot through with swirling streaks of green and blue, and aglow with a ghostly phosphorescence.

Far below, where the island rose sheer and tall from of the depths of Superior, waves crashed against stone. The sound echoed in Geo's mind like a summons.

The dragons roared, flying toward him in the gloaming.

"There!" shrieked Kaya. "I see him! I shall devour him!"

"Back Kaya! He is mine!" snarled Gibber.

"One day I shall eat you!" Kaya screamed. "When Nimue's Gift is mine!"

"You will never have it!" bellowed Gibber and flew

snapping at Kaya.

Gibber and Kaya began a battle in the sky. The other two dragons veered around them and continued on towards Geo.

Geo leapt from the cave, shimmering as he plummeted through the air to the water below.

He plunged into Superior and darted forward underwater like a shining fish.

He looked up through the surface of the water to see a blast of fire scorch the cliff face where he had been diving through the air just moments before.

Geo swam on, skimming below the foaming waves. He rolled over onto his back to scan the sky as he cut through the water.

A dark form flew in the air above him. Geo turned, and it turned with him, tracking his course.

My glowing body! Geo realized.

At the same instant, the dragon that followed him from the sky folded its wings and dove toward the water at Geo.

Geo arched his back and turned downward, streaking for the depths. The dragon crashed into the water above him but Geo was already gone, far below in the deep and swimming away as fast as he could.

Another dragon plunged into the water to his side. Geo turned to watch it and was startled to see how well it swam. With its wings tucked close to its body it undulated through the water like a great sea serpent.

But it could not swim like Geo. He wasn't even sure he was swimming. It felt more like he was water itself, melded into it, flowing with it and through it.

The dragon caught sight of Geo's shimmering glow and turned toward him, snaking through the water in pursuit.

Geo strained for speed and dove still deeper, penetrating beyond the depth that the light from the setting sun could reach.

All was dark. He could see only as far as his own phosphorescence cast its glow. But he hardly needed sight to navigate. He could feel the motion of the water around him, feel the pull of the rising moon on the deep, feel the eddy and swirl of water around submerged stones, and feel the swiftness where currents rushed through narrow channels between islands. And beyond all these, like a magnet drawing him, was the great deep: the dark, silent heart of Superior, far out from all land where starlight shown only on the ceaseless heaving of the waves.

He hungered for that unknown deep, and knew he could lose himself there for an age and still not explore all its mysteries.

No, he thought. *I cannot. Not now. Alette. I must give Alette time. I must keep the dragons close to me, pursuing me.*

Geo swam back to the surface and started moving toward shore.

One of the dragons that swam underwater caught sight of his glimmering phosphorescence and slithered after him. The other dragon in the water fell in with it, swimming in pursuit of Geo's shining form.

Geo skimmed fast just below the surface where he was sure the flicker of his glowing, liquid body would be visible from the air. Rolling over onto his back to look up at the sky, he reached out a hand that broke the surface of the water, slicing through the plane where sea and sky met, sending up a sparkling, cascading wake.

Through the rippling face of Lake Superior he saw a dragon, dark and massive, wheel around in the sky to come after him. Then another swooped down, almost knocking the first from the air as it fought to reach Geo first. It opened its mouth and shot a blast of fire at Geo.

Geo dove again into the deep. The flames slammed hissing into the waves, roiling the water above him.

Let the chase begin, Geo thought.

They were all with him, all pursuing, all eager to seize Nimue's Gift for themselves.

The sun sank low in the sky and the horizon flared red with the sunset. Geo wove back and forth through the saltless sea, darting now to the surface to flash bright, then streaking once more into the deep to avoid diving talons and spewing fire. Then from the depths he would emerge in a new place, tracing an erratic course that wended always to the west, away from where Alette sailed *The Morning Star*.

Chapter 15

Toward the Summit

From Alette's research notes:

*King Arthur was despised by his wife, Queen
Guenevere. He was the noblest man of his age, brave
and bold, generous and kind, valiant and strong, but
she would never love him.*

Still, she married him.

*She married him because Arthur was King,
because Arthur was handsome, and because Arthur
had more riches, and more honor, than any other man
in the realm. And she married him for the crown he
alone could bestow.*

Above all, she wanted to be Queen.

*So Guenevere took from Arthur the crown, and
with it Arthur gave her his own heart, but that she
never valued, and she never gave Arthur her heart.*

*And by her falseness of heart she broke all the
realm.*

*She sought illicit liaisons with other men and
through them did great harm. By one affair, she drove
from Arthur the powerful prince Sir Launcelot, who
had been one of Arthur's chief supports, and with
Launcelot went all his men-at-arms.*

*Then, when war called Arthur across the sea,
Guenevere took Mordred as her consort and put on his*

head King Arthur's own crown, the very crown that he had entrusted to her care when he departed.

Mordred, who was the son of Morgan Le Fay, King Arthur's great enemy. Morgan Le Fay was an evil enchantress and she hated Arthur. She tried time and again to kill Arthur by various schemes of treachery and was always eager to do him any injury she could. And it was her son that Guenevere now embraced.

Guenevere and Mordred seized all power in the realm and ruled as King and Queen in Arthur's absence. They had no fear, for they expected Arthur, bereft of the help of Launcelot, never to return from bloody war.

But Arthur did return.

And at word of his coming, Mordred and Guenevere trembled.

They hastened to gather a great host, intending to prevent Arthur's landing.

When Arthur's ships appeared, Mordred was at the shore with an army to drive them back into the sea. When their ships could not land, King Arthur and his knights jumped from the ships into the plunging waves. Mordred attacked them as they tried to wade ashore, thinking no man could fight from amid the sea and prevail.

But Mordred did not reckon on the kind of man Arthur was, or the kind of men they were who followed him.

They were fell warriors, battle hardened and grim, who knew well their trade. Even from the midst

of the sea they broke the ranks of Mordred's army,
won to the shore, and routed their enemies.

Mordred fled. He ran across the land and
gathered a new army as he went, trading in the
currency of lies. Mordred promised the greedy
whatever their hearts longed for. Extravagant and
base were his offers. And well he could afford to
promise anything, for his empty words cost him
nothing and he expected that those who took up arms
against Arthur had but little chance of living to ever
try collecting on the promises he made them. He cared
not if they died. All the better if they did, so long as
they killed Arthur first.

See *The History of the Kings of Britain*, by
Geoffrey of Monmouth (circa 1130 A.D.); see
Roman de Brut, by Wace (circa 1150 A.D.); see
Le Morte D'Arthur, by Sir Thomas Malory (circa
1450 A.D.); see *The Life of Merlin*, by Geoffrey of
Monmouth (circa 1150 A.D.); see *Brut*, by
Layamon (circa 1190 A.D.)

Geo's glowing, translucent body slipped through
the water like moonlight. Near the coast he turned to
swim parallel with the shore, heading further north,
seeking a river to take him inland.

Once, something large and strange ghosted up
alongside him, staying just beyond the range of his

vision. It mirrored his movements, turning as Geo turned, diving or rising with Geo as he swam down toward the bottom or up to the surface, always maintaining its distance just beyond the edge of sight. Then, just as suddenly as it had come out of the deep, it sank back again and was gone.

Geo continued up the coast until he felt a rush of warmer water burrowing into the cold of Superior and knew a river emptied there into the great lake.

He wanted to lead the dragons off the lake and into the wild lands of the northern forest. But with the phosphorescent sheen of his liquid body he feared he would not be able to keep hidden and evade the dragons within the confines of a river. So he wanted to enter a river and get upstream before they knew he had left the lake. Then he would call the dragons once again when he had reached the interior.

To do that he would lead the dragons past the mouth of the river and then double back. So now he continued further north and left the river behind.

When he was well past the point of the river's opening into Superior he came to the surface and raced just beneath the rippling, moonlight speckled waves, where the glow of his watery body would be revealed. Red fire flashed across the sky as the dragons spotted him and wheeled in his direction.

When Geo saw them coming he dove down deep, reversed course, and shot through the water as fast as he could back to the river. Behind him he heard the stinging and hissing of water scalded by a blast of dragon fire.

He reached the mouth of the river and turned into its rushing current, passing within its narrow banks and leaving the vastness of the great deep behind him.

The river was swift and strong, leaping and dancing over stones as it plunged down from the hills.

Geo swam upriver until he came to a tributary. It was smaller and colder, coming from higher up in the cliffs and headlands. He turned into it, moving farther into the wilderness.

He followed the tributary into the hills, its clear water sparkling with starlight.

Geo turned into other branchings and tributaries as he came to them, always seeking pathways to the high country. The streams became smaller and shallower as he made his way higher until at last he could swim no farther. He stood to wade onward and was surprised at how his shimmering, flowing legs sliced easily through the water. He almost glided along, moving faster through the midst of the stream than he could run on land in his own body.

On he went as the stream narrowed and became shallower and shallower, leading finally to a broad, shallow pool high in the rocky hills, the stream's rising and headwater, a natural rock basin cut into a stone outcropping below the hill's summit. The pool glistened in the starlight.

But as Geo looked at it, beautiful and shimmering with silvery light, he was confused. He could feel the presence of a great body of water somewhere nearby and knew this little basin could not be it.

Moonlight sparkled on a wet slick oozing down a

rock wall that formed one side of the basin. The wall overhung the pool and from its bottom edge trickling water dripped with a tinkling splash into the pool, making ripples in the moonlight.

A subterranean reservoir, Geo realized, *somewhere within that mass of stone.*

He ached to enter it.

Air was wicking moisture from him and the wind in the high hills stung as it cut into him. If he were to remain in this liquid form much longer he must fully submerge himself again.

It was time to transform back, time to call the dragons.

Geo stepped from the pool, his shimmering, watery body materializing again into bone and sinew as he tread onto the rocky shelf at the pool's edge.

He stood for a moment under the stars beside the lonely pool. Pines shook and creaked in the wind. The air was rich with the scent of their resin.

He looked at the sky. The moon was far along in its course. It was well after midnight. A new day had begun sometime while he swam through the depths of Superior and made his way through the twisting streams of the northland.

He reached for the golden case, felt its tingling energy, and opened it. He took out *The Book of Merlin*. He would bring the dragons to these hills, off the lake and farther from Alette.

He opened the book and power erupted into the night.

Chapter 16

Into the Shadows

From Alette's research notes:

In the end, Arthur was betrayed by a serpent.

Word of Arthur's need came to Launcelot. When he heard how Guenevere and Mordred had usurped Arthur's throne, Launcelot was full of sorrow and remorse, for Arthur was the most noble man of his age and a true King. Launcelot repented of his conflict with Arthur and sent word to Arthur that he was hastening to his aid with all his men-at-arms.

Meanwhile, Mordred sought a temporary truce with Arthur to gather yet more troops before again facing Arthur in battle, so fearful was Mordred of Arthur's might.

For his part, having received word from Launcelot that he hurried to his succor, Arthur said he would agree to a truce, that he might await the coming of Launcelot with his knights, for well Arthur knew that with Launcelot's support he would prevail utterly over Mordred.

To conclude the terms of their truce, Arthur and Mordred met together with their captains in the middle of a great field, within sight of the two armies arrayed against each other on opposite sides of the field.

Then in the midst of the parley in the middle of the field a great, poisonous serpent suddenly appeared. From whence it had come, none could ever say. But suddenly it was there, and seeing it, a knight drew his sword to kill the serpent.

When the two armies saw a naked sword drawn in the middle of the field each thought the other guilty of treachery and both armies charged into battle.

Thus was the final battle commenced. In it, Arthur killed Mordred with his own hands, but Mordred wounded Arthur with a mortal wound.

Queen Guenevere fled and hid herself and no one ever knew what became of her after that.

See *The History of the Kings of Britain*, by Geoffrey of Monmouth (circa 1130 A.D.); see *Roman de Brut*, by Wace (circa 1150 A.D.); see *Le Morte D'Arthur*, by Sir Thomas Malory (circa 1450 A.D.); see *The Life of Merlin*, by Geoffrey of Monmouth (circa 1150 A.D.); see *Brut*, by Layamon (circa 1190 A.D.)

Geo read *The Fourth Cycle* aloud from *The Book of Merlin*:

> *Sun and moon rule day and night*
> *Give me their power of dark and light*

There was the swirl of power, its inward rushing, its soaking into Geo like a wave seeping into the sand of a beach, and when it had been absorbed into him, without knowing what he was doing, Geo reached out his hand to a shaft of moonlight and watched as it bent to swirl around his fingers. He moved his hand in a circle and the moonlight followed. He cupped his hand to gather the trailing swirl of light, then closed his fingers around it and squeezed, pressing the light into a tight ball, feeling it contract under his grip.

Geo flung the ball of light into the sky and it sailed up into the night where it burst like a great, shining bubble in the dark.

Geo looked again at *The Book of Merlin*. The page where *The Fourth Cycle* had been was now blank. He turned to the next page and read aloud *The Fifth Cycle*:

> *Through the firmament to soar as king*
> *Transform me now to fly on wing*

The energy began once more to sweep faster around him, turned inward, penetrated into him, vibrating through his muscles, searing into his bones, changing him.

All at once it released him and Geo threw out great wings and leapt into the air.

He wheeled in the sky and glided in a circle around the shallow pool, watching it sparkle in the moonlight beneath him. Geo spotted a perch in a giant pine tree nearby and swooped down to land.

He shook himself and felt feathers shifting over his

body. He edged closer to the trunk of the tree, moving sideways along the branch on which he roosted, and hid himself beneath thick pine boughs.

It was not a moment too soon.

Suddenly the pines shook as a massive, dark form thundered from sky and pummeled into the earth.

Seconds later another crash further downstream reverberated through the forest. In quick succession two other dragons struck hard into the hillside on each side of the stream, one so close that the tree where Geo hid shivered from the impact.

Gibber rushed forward into the starlight at the edge of the pool. "Burn the stream!" he shrieked in his rasping voice and shot an enormous blast of fire that raked the shallow water and sent clouds of steam hissing into the air.

"Strafe the water!" Gibber commanded. "Don't let him slip through!"

The other dragons pounded forward, shaking the forest, and hurled jets of flame at the stream.

The intensity of the dragon fire lit the night. Geo gathered darkness and held it close about himself, shrouding himself in shadow.

The dragons stamped into the bubbling, steaming water, searching.

"He is not here, Gibber," said Kaya.

"Keep searching! He is near!" Gibber ordered, then turned from the water and stalked into the forest.

"You cannot hide from us!" Gibber yelled. "We will smell you out! We will find you and I will consume you!"

114

The other dragons spread out and began searching around the stream and pool, peering through the gloom, sniffing.

Suddenly one of the dragons roared and tramped its feet, making the forest quake.

The dragon stopped just as suddenly and stood waiting, silent, listening.

He's trying to panic me, Geo realized, *to flush me out.*

The din from the dragon's stomping and roaring faded and the woods subsided again into the small sounds of the night.

The dragons resumed their prowling.

"Or," Gibber spoke again, "I can offer you something. Let us make a deal, shall we? I will give you something Merlin would never give you. And where is Merlin, eh? He sends you to fight us, but where is he? He does not fight. Have you wondered why? Look at all those he has sent against us. Launcelot, dead. Servause, dead. Bors, dead. Beowulf, dead. Sigurd, dead."

Gibber paused.

"*Yet Merlin lives on*," the dragon hissed. "Oh yes, he says he'll give you what he calls *weapons*, *gifts*. He *says* he'll give you what you *need* to face us. But if he has everything that's needed, why doesn't he face us himself? And why do all those he sends against us end up the same way? *Dead.*"

The other dragons continued prowling, hunting their quarry while Gibber talked.

"Do you really think Merlin has offered you *all* his secrets?" Gibber asked. "Did you ask him how it is that he still lives? After all these ages? And after so many others have died? Think about that. Think about what he keeps from you, what he keeps for himself. Ask yourself why he withholds secrets from you."

One of the dragons, Madne, found the place where the trickle issued from the rock, the wellspring of the stream. He began sniffing and scratching at the stone.

"Gibber, he is not here," Madne said. "There is water underground here, joined no doubt by subterranean channels to the great water. What if he has followed the dark pathways of the hidden water back to the saltless sea?"

"No, Madne," Gibber answered, "he is near."

Gibber raised his head and smelled the air. "There!" he screamed suddenly and roared, flinging his head wildly about, looking into the night.

Geo remained still as stone, wrapped in shadow.

The dragons were poised, ready to spring, listening and peering through the moonlit forest for the least flicker of motion.

"Show yourself, coward!" Gibber screamed.

Geo watched the huge black mass of the dragon in the darkness and thought of the Rock Wizard's painting on the cave wall.

They can be slain, he told himself. *They must be slain.*

Gibber moved on.

"There are other powers, you know," Gibber said softly. "Powers greater than what Merlin can offer. Or did he not tell you that? Did he not tell you why he hides while he sends others out? Why he seeks to kill us? If it is power you want, then come to me. I will give you power. Then we can go together to Merlin to *take* from him the secrets he withholds, the secret to life, *life forever*."

Gibber paused and looked around the forest.

"Think on that," Gibber purred in a seductive voice. "To *live forever*. How would you like that? That is what Merlin has. That is what he keeps for himself. That is what he will not share. Why should he have it and you not? Join us, and together we can take it!"

"Let us make a deal," Gibber went on. "This is the bargain I offer you: you give me Nimue's Gift, and I will give you *life . . . forever*."

Gibber raised his nose to smell the breeze.

"And . . ." the dragon began again, "I will let your woman live, also. Yes, we have not forgotten her. Though I see that you have taken Nimue's Gift for yourself. Very clever of you. Very shrewd. I think we are not so different after all, you and I. But still, I think her life is not entirely unimportant, is it?"

There was another pause as Gibber crept through the dark.

"And I will give you power," Gibber resumed. "Power such as mine. My STRENGTH. My FIRE. My SIZE. Then together we can obtain the ultimate secrets from Merlin. Why be Merlin's servant when you can BE HIS MASTER?"

The dragon reared up on his hind legs and roared, blasting a great shower of flame into the sky.

"JOIN ME OR DIE!" he screamed.

But even before Gibber's shriek faded into the night

a rumble, great and deep, came over the horizon, streaking toward them louder and louder.

Fighter jets flew overhead shaking the night!

"We must leave!" Kaya yelled.

"He is not here!" screamed another.

"Krule is right," said Madne. "He is not here. He must have gone into the water under the rock. He is somewhere underground now, we must wait until he comes back to the surface."

Gibber growled and did not move.

"We cannot allow *them* to find us," said Kaya, looking at the sky.

"He must be here!" bellowed Gibber. "We felt the power! We saw the sphere of light!"

But as Geo watched, he could already perceive the great bulk of the dragons subsiding, shrinking, as all four began scaling back to human dimensions.

"And what if we are dragged into the light?" asked Kaya. "We must remain hidden. We must tear down the tower."

"Besides, I don't think he understands Nimue's Gift," said Madne.

"Quiet," commanded Gibber, his voice almost human now as the transformation proceeded. "He may be listening. What he does not know is to our advantage."

"But look how he ran!" said Madne.

"Yes," answered Gibber, stepping forward into a shaft of moonlight. The pale, silvery beam illuminated the warping and kneading of Gibber's face as it was molded in the process of transmogrification back into human shape.

"Yes," Gibber repeated, smiling. "Fear is a beautiful thing. He will defeat himself with his own fear."

The fighter jets flew overhead again.

"We will find him," Gibber said. "He is close, I can feel it. When he accesses the power again, we will have him."

The four dragon-men, now fully returned to human form, laughed and moved off through the forest, heading down the mountain.

Agawa Rock Pictograph on Lake Superior, found with the directions given to Henry Schoolcraft on a birchbark scroll

Chapter 17

Dawn

From Alette's research notes:

Saint Brendan and his monks crossed the great salt sea to a new land. One day as they explored along the coasts and islands of the new land a huge and hideous monster appeared in the sky, flying toward them on enormous wings. Saint Brendan told his brother monks not to fear and prayed to Our Lord for deliverance. When Saint Brendan's prayer was finished a beautiful bird, exceedingly large and splendid to behold, with dazzling white plumage, was seen streaking through the sky toward the monster. The monster was many times larger than the beautiful bird but the bird had no fear of the monster and attacked it in the middle of the air, slashing it with its talons and beak, diving again and again at the monster. The monster roared and turned to fight the white bird and a great battle took place in the sky. The white bird slew the monster and it fell crashing into the sea, dead.

See *The Voyage of Saint Brendan the Navigator* (circa 800 A.D.)

From Alette's research notes:

"When I founded the Round Table," said Merlin, "I made it round as a sign for the world, which is round, for the fellowship of the Round Table and the deeds of its knights are to serve all the world."

And truly it was so, for knights of the Round Table roved far and wide over the wild seas, to many lands strange and unknown, and did battle there with perilous beasts.

See *Le Morte D'Arthur*, by Sir Thomas Malory (circa 1450 A.D.)

Geo waited a long time, wrapped in shadow, listening. The sounds of the night were sharp and clear in his ears. And his eyes in this new form could pick out fine details far away, even in the dim light of the moon and stars. He also discovered that through his feet and feathers he had keen awareness of vibrations and subtleties of wind that brought him all manner of information.

The voices of the Spartoi and their footsteps had long since faded from the forest, but still Geo waited. He remembered the stealth they had shown in springing their trap at the stream. All four had circled, silent and unseen, high in the sky, surrounding the place from which the power had emanated. Then suddenly they dropped from the sky, cutting off flight in every direction. If he had not already been away they would have had him.

So now he stayed hidden, and wondered at the dragons' words. *What did Merlin tell you . . . What did Merlin offer you . . . Merlin is alive . . . Merlin has life that continues forever . . .*

It was what Alette told him the legends said.

Could it be true? Did Merlin still live? If so, where was he?

The night reached its darkest when the moon's course through the sky was almost complete.

It was the time to travel unseen.

Geo moved out on the branch until he was clear of overhanging pine boughs, unfolded his great wings, and launched himself from his perch. His wings beat the air with tremendous strength and power. He flew high and fast, soaring over the forest. As he went, he continued to hold shadow close to him, enveloping himself in darkness as he flew. Wrapped in the inky shadows of night, he could not see his avian body, but knew he must be large.

Wind buffeted him and he turned into it, letting it carry him higher as he glided through the dark sky.

He flew a long time. Below, the forests began to thin, giving way first to pasture, then to cultivated fields. Far away on the horizon he could see the restless, sparkling waters of Lake Superior reflecting the last of the night's starlight.

He passed over a farmhouse with a huge, ancient maple growing in its yard. Nearby was a big red barn. The yard was enclosed by a white picket fence. Ploughed fields lay beyond the farmyard and a ribbon of dirt road ran from the farm off into the distance. Everything was quiet and peaceful.

Geo was exhausted. The farmstead offered a sheltered refuge for a few hours' sleep.

In a few quick circles he descended and landed in the giant maple tree. He ruffled his feathers, smoothed them, adjusted his perch, and settled himself. For a long time he sat still and silent, listening and watching. Children's toys were in the yard. A doghouse stood in a corner of the picket fence across from the tree, the dog asleep. Everything was at rest.

Geo relaxed his mind. He let go of the shadow and darkness he was holding close to himself, allowing them to drift away. He closed his eyes and slept.

* * *

The scrape of an opening window woke him. Geo blinked, alert, poised.

He heard kitchen noises coming from the open window. A warm, yellow light spilled out.

The color of the sky told him dawn was not far off. He could not have slept long.

The sound of a coffee pot gurgling reached his ears and the aroma of hot coffee wafted out into the chilly morning.

From the open window Geo heard steps descending

a wooden staircase within the house. Then a man's voice, drowsy and warm, said, "Good morning, beautiful woman."

"Good morning to you, handsome man," a woman's voice answered.

There was the sound of a kiss.

"Cup of coffee?" the woman asked.

"Sounds heavenly," the man said.

Geo heard coffee poured into a mug.

Then a pause, the thunk of the mug on a kitchen table, and, "Ahh," the man said appreciatively, "that's good coffee."

Bacon sizzled in a pan. Its aroma made Geo's stomach tighten. He realized he was ravenously hungry.

"How about bacon and eggs this morning?" the woman asked.

"Mmm, my favorite," the man said. "Shall I make the toast?"

"That would be a wonderful help," the woman answered.

More kitchen noises followed, along with low-voiced, still-waking-up conversation. Then he heard new steps on the wooden staircase, these lighter, and a new voice entered, a child's voice.

"Momma, can I have my morning snuggle?" the little voice asked.

"Good morning, Honey," the woman answered in a tone that touched Geo's heart. "I was hoping for a snuggle. You come right over here."

The sun rose, casting the long shadows of morning across the thick, soft grass of the lawn.

Geo was tired and hungry, but he was seized with an urgent desire to leave. He could not let his presence here jeopardize these people. He could not risk bringing the dragons to this place. There was something sacred here, something to be protected, and he dared not endanger it.

He spread his wings and took to the sky.

It's not just Alette and I, Geo thought. *Even if we could outrun the dragons indefinitely, they'd still be out there.*

Geo wanted sleep. He wanted food. But he flew on.

Why did The Book of Merlin come to me? he wondered.

He hadn't sought it, but it was given to him. Why? What should he do with it?

Geo shook his head to clear his thoughts and flew on through the cool morning air. He would find a new place to sleep. He would rest. He would find food. Then, while still far away from the cabin, he would open *The Book of Merlin* and complete the last of its Cycles. That would draw the dragons. When it did, he would dash to Alette as fast as he could.

He would keep his promise.

Then there would be a chance to decide on their course of action.

Geo's flight took him over an inland lake that reflected the clear blue sky back up to him. He looked down into its shining, still surface and saw his own reflection in the sparkling water.

It took his breath away.

He was beautiful.

He had never seen such a bird. He was huge and shining white, with brilliant, dazzling plumage and sleek lines.

An instant later a ripple beneath the surface of the water galvanized his attention and focused all his senses. Acting on instinct, he dove at the water, razor sharp talons extended. In a flash his talons dipped into the water, closed, and he was streaking back into the sky with an enormous fish clutched in his grip.

He found a rocky promontory, landed and ate. Then he returned to the lake to hunt again, over and over, each time bringing his catch back to the high, lonely rock to eat. When at last his hunger was sated he flew on once more until he found a place to sleep in a crag of stone sheltered from the wind. There he settled himself, listened to the howl of the wind over the high country, and closed his eyes.

As he drifted into sleep images swirled through his mind, filling the misty space between waking and dreams, images of Mr. Wygar packing up his cabin, of a shaggy bear roaring in a mountain meadow, of a stag illuminated in a flash of piercing Light, and as he saw them it seemed the wind whispered in his ears *Merlin, Merlin, Merlin.*

Chapter 18

The Last Cycle

From Alette's research notes:

Merlin took the form of a great and mighty stag, with enormous antlers, and came to the emperor. The emperor was filled with wonder to see such a magnificent animal walking toward him completely unafraid and approaching as if with a purpose.

Then Merlin, while still in the form of a stag, hailed the emperor in human speech, and the emperor and all those with him were utterly astounded.

"Who are you?" asked the emperor to the stag.

"You will know that in due season," Merlin answered, "but what you must know now is that war is upon you. Arm yourself! Prepare for battle while you still can!"

Then the stag departed from the emperor and slipped into the woods and ran among the deep places of the forest.

See *The Story of Merlin*, by Anonymous (circa 1215 A.D.)

A cold wind woke Geo. He kept his eyes closed and felt the wind moving over him, brisk and sumptuous as it riffled his feathers.

He took some moments to enjoy it, resting and breathing deeply of the cool, fresh air. When he finally opened his eyes he saw that it was evening again. He had slept through the day. Once more the world was dusky with the deep purples and violet blues of twilight.

He must be going. He took one last slow, deep breath, shook out his great wings, stretched, and launched into the sky.

He flew on and on as night settled over the land, heading away from civilization into the back country.

After long hours soaring over unbroken forest he saw a clearing open to the sky below him. He circled it, alert for signs of danger, and when he found none, swooped down to land. He began transforming back into his human form even as his taloned claws stretched out to touch the ground. For a moment as he came to rest on the turf of long, tangled grasses, he was half-man and half-winged creature while the strange ripples of shifting worked through his muscles. It felt distinctly odd to have your flesh molded like clay in the process of moving from one shape into another. He wondered if such transformations were the basis for mythical creatures like the Centaur or Minotaur. Perhaps shapeshifters had been spied in the process of transmogrification, caught half-way between one form and another, giving rise to the legends.

The last of the shifting passed. He held up a hand and saw his fingers fully human again. He clenched and unclenched his fist. It felt good to be back in his own skin.

He looked up at the bright, shining moon. It was already past midnight.

He peered around the dark clearing. He was in the middle of vast, trackless wilderness on the other side of Lake Superior from the cabin of Alette's father. It was a good place to finish *The Book of Merlin* and lure the dragons to before making his dash to Alette.

Wind blew through the field. The only sounds were the creak of the surrounding trees and the rustle of swaying grass.

There was no reason to wait.

Geo reached for the case, felt the charge of power run up through his fingers as he touched it, and took out *The Book of Merlin*.

He opened the book's cover and the great wave of crackling energy poured out from it.

Geo scanned the sky. No sign of the dragons yet. He didn't know how far away they were, but knew they wouldn't delay long in responding to the call of the power.

He turned through the pages of *The Book of Merlin* and saw that only one remained, the only page that now showed any writing to him. He reached out his hand and gathered a spark of starlight. He held it in his fingers to illuminate the final page. It was titled: *The Sixth Cycle*.

Geo read the words of the final *Cycle* aloud:

On the earth walk beasts of many kinds
Let the form of each now be mine

The power from the book channeled itself into a stream that swirled around him. Patterns formed and broke as the power rushed faster and faster until it became a flashing blur and spiraled inward converging on him. It penetrated into his body, travelling in waves through him.

Geo's vision changed rapidly, as if he were seeing a series of slides click by one after another. But the changing images weren't pictures of different scenes. It was the same field and forest that lay before him, but seen through different sets of changing eyes, each with its own perception, its own sight, that showed different aspects of the one reality. Some saw the night brilliantly, others only dimly, and through some he saw new colors he had never known before and strange forms of radiance beyond his understanding.

His perspective also changed as he grew or shrank from one form into another, being lost one moment amid the blades of grass and then rising up the next to tower over the field. His senses of smell and hearing were altered with each transformation and his bones and muscles ached as they were twisted from shape to shape.

It was too much. He became dizzy and disoriented. He wanted it to stop, he wanted to break free from the power, but it held him in its grip and worked relentlessly through him, refusing to set him loose, molding him from one form into another.

And then with a great inward rush the last of the power was absorbed into him and everything became still and silent.

He stood for a moment, dazed. His body trembled. His nose quivered and his ears twitched. His brain was inundated by alien senses gathering scents and sounds he had not been aware of in his human form. His vision was now weak, discerning only indistinct shades of gray. But he hardly needed sight, so keen were his other senses. Whiskers, which he realized he now possessed, brought him information from the movement of the air and registered traces of heat and energy and motion all around him.

He felt four long, thin, powerful legs beneath him, light and strong and ready to leap away in an instant.

He looked down and saw his body shaped into the strong, lithe form of a deer. He was a stag with great antlers.

His nose wrinkled at a foul scent carried on the night wind. The dragons. From the scent and the breeze he knew they were still a long way off but drawing near rapidly.

Before the conscious thought to flee could even form in his mind he was already darting away, running hard and fast, moving by instinct, almost by feel, through the meadow and into the trees.

He leapt over roots and fallen logs and dashed through whipping branches as he sped through the forest.

Behind him a blast of red fire shot through the sky. The earth shuddered from the tremendous impact of dragons crashing into the ground.

But Geo was already away, ghosting swift and silent through the forest like a sylvan spirit in the form of a mighty stag.

Manana Island, Maine, where Saint Brendan is said to have landed, seen from Monhegan Island; rocks on Manana Island bear ancient runes of unknown origin

Chapter 19

The Flight

From Alette's research notes:

> *See the stag! Noble creature! Standing against the sky with his mighty antlers shining in the light of the rising sun, resplendent in majesty!*

See *The Poetic Edda* (circa 900 A.D.)

It was an experience Geo never forgot, that flight through the forest at night. He could feel his whole body aquiver, alive with tension, like the string of a guitar drawn tight and struck to resonate in perfect pitch. He was filled with joy at the power coursing through his muscles and thrilled at the pinpoint precision of his hooves amid the bracken as he maneuvered through the trees.

He was guided by scent and sight and hearing and the quiver of his whiskers, but even more than these by something else, something he could not name: a heightened sensitivity to the ever-fluctuating tremors of creation. He had an awareness of ceaseless oscillations along threads of consciousness and mind running between and among all living things, connecting them one to another. As Geo sprinted through the dark forest he was not moving through empty space, but amid a tangled network of interwoven strands, the vibration along any one of which was felt in those around it, extending outward in concentric circles of perception.

He realized it was something he had felt all his life, but less distinctly, less powerfully, than he did now, as if he had been aware of it before only as a distant light seen dimly through a haze of fog. It was this sense that had made the hairs of his arm stand on end when the bear stalked him. Now, in the form of a deer, the awareness of this other sense was acute and strong.

And through this unnamed sense he felt the presence of the dragons. All of the forest did, and all fled as fast as they could, Geo along with the rest.

Yet even with the presence of the dragons so close it was exhilarating to race through the moonlit forest, guided by this new awareness, with the scents and sounds of the night rushing past him in the speed of his flight.

Then, as he ran on, a new sensation came to Geo. It was an undercurrent of thought, of consciousness, like an unseen stream of spirit running through the forest, that he was somehow a part of, even as he remained distinct within it. He sensed the presence of others of his kind, of other deer, a herd, and veered to join it.

He felt the skittishness and panic the dragons had caused in them. They had scattered and run through the night as he had and now they were joining together again, reforming as a group, drawn to each other through the web of their shared consciousness. Geo allowed himself to be guided along the channels of the herd's intermingling thought and let its common pool of mind meld his motions to join in unison with the other deer. Even as he did, he felt a separation from the stream of their shared thought, as if he were a leaf, a stick, something separate carried along in the stream, rather than a part of the stream itself. Somehow he was not able to fully enter into the shared mind of the herd.

As the herd reformed, he was aware of first one deer, then another, gliding through the forest glades alongside him. As they banded together they followed a great stag who led them on and on until the dragons' presence had been left behind, and still the great stag ran on.

The herd was tired, but the great stag continued, so they did as well, following and struggling to keep up.

Finally, as morning approached, the great stag slackened his pace. The other deer slowed, hooves dragging, sides heaving as they panted for breath. When the great stag at last halted they were near the shores of a lake. The other deer gathered around the great stag, their legs trembling with exhaustion. Geo stood with them, his own legs shaking like those of the others.

At the lake's edge his senses were flooded by the smell of water and good things to eat, of sweet grasses and succulent tree bark.

The great stag had led them to a good place.

And Geo knew that this was the great stag's herd, that the great stag was the King of this clan of deer.

The other deer stood around the Stag King, waiting on him, holding back from the water and from feeding while the Stag King listened and sniffed the air and scanned the shore and reached out with that other sense to feel along the interconnecting strands of awareness for any telltale quiver that whispered of danger.

All was peaceful and quiet.

Finally the Stag King lowered his head and approached the water to drink. Then rest of the herd came forward to drink and spread out to begin feeding, Geo with them.

A soft golden light fell shining on the lake as dawn broke.

The deer grazed, paused to lift their heads to look and listen, then grazed again. After feeding they began to make beds for themselves in the tall, soft grass, and lay down in ones and twos. Acting on instinct, Geo moved in a circle through the high grass, breaking stalks and matting down the grass to make a bed for himself. Then he lay down upon the fragrant stems and was soon fast asleep.

Chapter 20

Dreams

Based on a quote of Dr. Dan Burke:

Not all the thoughts in your head are your own . . .

From Alette's research notes:

The first rule of war is to admit when you are at war.

See *The Poetic Edda* (circa 900 A.D.)

Strange dreams floated through Geo's mind, fading one into another, swirling through the mist of sleep. Images of forests and fens blended into scenes of sunlit meadows where wildflowers stirred in the breeze; winter snows of white blurred into brilliantly colored autumn leaves bright against blue skies; there were glimpses of distant valleys seen from high mountain scarps. Geo realized he was viewing memories of things he had never seen. They were the dreams of the deer who lay sleeping around him, drifting by in the stream of their shared consciousness.

Some were dreams handed down from ages past. Some were dreams of young deer not yet born who slept yet in their mothers' wombs.

In one dream Geo saw an old doe with many seasons of life behind her and a young fawn still new to the world. With the uncanny knowledge of dreams Geo knew that the doe was the fawn's mother. The fawn had lagged behind, unable to keep up with the herd, and his mother stayed back with him, urging him on. Then in the dream Geo heard the howl of wolves. Yellow eyes appeared, glowing in the shadows of the forest, and they crept nearer. Wolves emerged from the gloom, slinking out of the darkness with fangs bared.

Suddenly a great stag burst into the midst of the wolves. The great stag slashed with its mighty antlers and struck out with sharp hooves. It had come back at the sound of the wolf howls and now scattered the wolves as it broke in among them like a storm.

Come! Quickly! the great stag commanded and led the doe and fawn bounding away through the forest.

The wolves recovered from the shock of the great stag's sudden assault and chased after them.

As the three deer ran they heard the howling of the wolves begin again behind them. Soon after came the crashing of the wolves through the forest, the terrible sound drawing closer and closer as the wolves gained on them.

Keep going! The great stag ordered, then wheeled

about and charged once more into the wolves, shattering their pursuit.

Again and again as the deer fled the great stag turned back on the snarling wolves, until at last the old doe and her fawn had made it safely away.

Other dreams came and the vision of the great stag melted into new images as the annals of the deer clan, the record of their deeds through generations, passed before the vision of Geo's mind.

Geo could not fully enter the dreams as the other deer did, but he watched them as they slipped past in the constantly moving stream of the deer's mingled spirit, the shared genius of the tribe, while remaining a rock standing out in the stream, within the stream but separate from it, something around which the stream parted and eddied.

The dream of the powerful stag who rescued the doe and fawn from the wolves did not simply glide past Geo as the others had. It stopped, swirling about the rock of Geo's consciousness, watching Geo as he watched the dreams of the others sweep by. Then the dream of the great stag also separated from the whirling current of dreams and disappeared.

A few moments later Geo was awakened by a deer standing over him. It watched Geo, sniffed him, prodded him with a hoof. Geo looked up and saw the Stag King.

You are not one of us, said the Stag King.

Afterward, when Geo looked back on this encounter, he tried to reconstruct how the deer communicated. It was partly through gesture, the raising and lowering of head or tail or the flick of whiskers. It was partly by sound. But more than these, it was through their shared pool of consciousness, an interchange that occurred along common pathways of awareness.

Years later Geo read of an experiment Benjamin Franklin conducted with an open jar of honey suspended by a string from the ceiling of a room. Franklin released an ant into the honey jar. The ant snatched some honey and scurried up the string, across the ceiling, down the wall, and away. Franklin left the jar suspended from the ceiling and when he came back later he found two long lines of marching ants, one that made its way up the wall and across the ceiling to scale down the string to the honey jar, the second making the return journey transporting honey collected from the jar back to their colony. The ants, Franklin concluded, had some means of communication about which we know nothing. So too, Geo learned, do other animals.

You smell like one of us, the Stag King said, *but you do not share our dreams; you are not one of us.*

No, Geo said, *I am not one of you.*

With sudden insight the Stag King said, *You are a shifter*.

A shifter? Geo asked, surprised that the deer should have a word for this power from *The Book of Merlin*.

They walk the wild, said the Stag King, *some coming and going between forms, others trapped in a shape they can no longer shed, having forsaken their given form and no longer living as a child of Creation.*

Geo immediately thought of Merlin.

Who are these shifters? he asked. *Do you know them?*

They live in the wild around us, here and there, we do not traffic with them, said the Stag King.

Have you ever heard of one named Merlin? Geo asked.

Merlin can shift, answered the King of the deer, *but he is not one of them. We will have communion with Merlin when he comes about.*

You know Merlin? Geo asked. *Can you take me to him?*

I know Merlin, the Stag King confirmed, *but I do not know where he is. Merlin comes and goes when he will. We never know when he will come or when he will go. Always he is engaged in The War, and we help him when we can, and he helps us when he can. Sometimes he comes to learn news of The War that we may have. Sometimes he comes to share with us his knowledge. And sometimes he comes to help us, to give us warning, or to heal us if sickness has come among us. Sometimes he comes only for the joy of running the forest. He is a friend to us and we allow him to run with us. But we have not seen him for many seasons now.*

War? Geo asked. *What war?*

The Stag King looked at Geo.

<u>The</u> *War*, the Stag King answered. *The War of all, The War raging around us now, do you not feel it? Do you not know it?*

But what war? I don't understand, Geo said.

141

The Stag King stood in silence considering Geo.

How then, he finally asked, *do you hope to win?*

Geo had no answer for him.

Was it you who brought the dragons to our forest? the Stag King asked.

Yes, Geo answered. *They hunt me.*

Then you fight the dragons with Merlin? asked the Stag King.

I fight the dragons, Geo said, *but not with Merlin. I have never met Merlin, though things from Merlin have come to me. But I want to find him. There is much I do not understand, there are many things I would like to ask him. May I run with you to seek Merlin?*

The Stag King shook his great head.

No, he said. *Merlin is not to be found. He reveals himself when he wishes. To seek Merlin is a fruitless quest. If he wishes for you to speak with him, he will find you. Otherwise, you will not speak with him. And my first duty is to those entrusted to my care. You are a danger to us.*

Geo suddenly recognized the Stag King from the dream he had seen of the great stag.

You are the stag from the dream, aren't you? Geo asked.

The Stag King nodded his head in confirmation. *Yes,* he said, *it was I in the dream.*

You saved the fawn and doe, Geo said.

No, the King said. *The doe was my mother. I was the fawn. And now it has come to me to protect our people, as once I was protected. I wish you well, but*

142

you must go from us. We will assist you in any way we can, for we too fight The War, but you cannot remain among us. May the Great King protect you in all your ways!

The Stag King stepped back and bowed his head in a gesture Geo understood to convey both farewell and command. It was time for him to leave.

He rose and returned the bow, bidding farewell to the Stag King.

Thank you, Geo said. *You have already helped me, and if I can ever assist you or any of your clan, I will.*

Geo turned and loped off along the shore of the lake. When he reached its far side he stopped and looked back over the water. The Stag King still stood on the far shore, watching him from across the lake. Once more the Stag King bowed. Geo returned the salute, turned, and ran off into the trees, leaving the shore and gliding into the forest.

Chapter 21

In the Northern Forest

From Alette's research notes:

The woman held the secret of life. Her name was Idunn, and she possessed a certain fruit which had the power to make the old grow young again. From whence and by what pathways it had come into her hand, none could say. The ancient tales do not tell. But howsoever it was, possess it she did, and she kept it in a wooden box. Then one day as she walked the northern forests where eagles fly and snows fall, Idunn's wooden box was stolen by the giants. A war was waged and Idunn's box was recovered, but too late. It had already been out in the world.

See *The Prose Edda* (circa 1200 A.D.)

Geo ran all morning through the forest, pausing only to eat and drink. Part of his mind thrilled at the new discoveries of the world coming to him through his new senses. Another part continued to turn over what he had learned: Merlin walked these forests. Merlin was alive. Merlin was at war. But what was The War? Why had Merlin said so little in his book?

If only he could find Merlin, talk to Merlin, ask Merlin.

But he could not.

So he ran on.

He had decided to remain hidden in the form of a deer amid the forest until he gained more distance from the last place he knew the dragons had been. When he was further away, and once darkness had fallen, he would transform to fly on the wind. Until then, he would remain lost in the northern forest as a stag running through the land.

He was in the cool shadows of the great forest, along the edge of a broad sunlit meadow, when he felt, through that strange sense of awareness he had in heightened measure as a deer, that something tracked him.

The tug of another's consciousness at a thread somewhere in the tangled web of awareness made Geo stop, poised and alert. He looked around.

It's across the field, he knew, feeling the presence, *whatever it is that follows me*.

Tentatively, Geo moved forward to the edge of the open meadow.

On the other side of the field he saw it: something large lumbering along the tree line. What it was, he could not say. Half man, half beast, larger than a bear, it shambled on two legs, bent forward, with long arms reaching below its knees and claw-like hands with massive fingers that ended in talons. Its legs were thick with knotted muscle, its face heavy and grotesque like a cathedral gargoyle. When Geo came to the edge of the tree line the creature stopped and stood still, watching him.

Geo could feel the intensity of its gaze from across the meadow.

It was hideous and unnatural, a creature like none Geo had ever seen, and it seemed very interested in him.

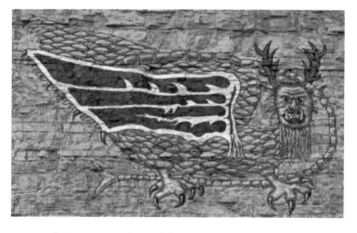

A modern recreation of the Piasa Bird, based on the description written by Father Marquette in his journal, in Alton, Illinois, near where the original was located

Chapter 22

Things that Walk the Wilderness

From Alette's research notes:

On Mont Saint-Michel there was a huge creature with the form like that of a man, but it was not a man. It was gigantic, and sought men to seize and rend apart to eat their flesh. Arthur met it in combat, and asked of it, "What are you? From whom are you born? Where do you come from on the earth?" It would not answer. "Why do you destroy the folk?" Arthur asked. Still, it would give him no answer, except to rush upon him in violence. King Arthur met its attack and in a terrible battle slew it to save his people.

See *Brut*, by Layamon (circa 1190 A.D.)

Geo stood at the edge of the tree line studying the creature as it stared at him.

It's not something of nature at all, Geo thought, *it's*

a shifted form.

A shifted form such as Merlin might take.

Could it be? He remembered the words of the Stag King: *if Merlin wishes you to speak with him, he will find you.*

This thing, whatever it was, had been tracking him.

Geo stepped forward out of the shade of the trees into the bright sunshine of the meadow, transforming back into human form as he moved.

The creature did not seem at all startled to see a deer change shape into a man before its eyes. It simply stood still, watching, waiting.

It was Geo who broke the silence, asking: "Merlin?"

The gigantic man-beast still remained silent, but took a cautious step toward Geo.

Geo shifted his stance, uneasy.

The creature took another step, beginning to walk slowly toward him. Geo moved along the edge of the meadow away from it, maintaining his distance from the creature as it came across the field.

Sunlight glinted off the golden case slung over his shoulder as Geo walked.

The creature stopped and stared. Then a gruesome leer that Geo supposed was its smile parted the creature's lips.

At last it spoke.

"Merlin," it said, repeating Geo's word in a voice that sounded like a growl.

"Who are you?" Geo asked.

The thing resumed its slow, shambling gait toward Geo.

"Who am I?" it asked with its grimace of a smile. "I am a seeker of treasures, as Merlin sought, and as Merlin found."

"What's your name?" Geo asked.

The thing shook its head *no* and did not answer.

"Does Merlin reveal himself?" it asked. "Not anymore does he. Yet Merlin still seeks, and Merlin still finds. You have treasure yourself. I would ask, who are you?"

"I have treasure?" Geo asked. "What treasure do you mean?"

"You have a treasure from Merlin, do you not?" the thing asked. "Even Nimue's Gift?"

"You know *The Book of Merlin*?" Geo asked.

The thing stopped and stood still looking at Geo. Then it threw its head back and roared with wicked laughter. "*The Book of Merlin*!" the thing cackled. "Oh, yes! This is treasure indeed! And delicious!"

It lowered its head again and looked at Geo.

"Merlin is indeed a seeker and a finder," it said, "one who discovers things that are hidden and lost. And Merlin is a giver of gifts. But not all that Merlin finds is his own, and not all the gifts he gives are his to give. Some things others possessed first. And sometimes Merlin loses the pretty things he has found."

"Do you know Merlin?" Geo asked.

"I have had dealings with Merlin," the thing said.

"Do you know where he is?"

"Do I know where he is?" the creature asked. "How should I answer that?"

"With the truth," Geo said.

Again the thing threw its head back and roared with laughter.

"Testy," it said in rejoinder. "Testy and impertinent. Be patient. I also am a seeker of treasure, and I too can be a giver of gifts. But it requires patience."

"Who are you?" Geo asked again.

The thing gave its leering smile and licked its lips with a huge, black tongue that was disgusting to see.

"As I have said," the creature answered in its deep, growling voice, "I am a seeker of treasure. A seeker and a finder. And I can be a dispenser of gifts, such as I have to give. And I will tell you what I see, what I think. I see one who possesses gifts from Merlin, yet who seeks Merlin. So I think that the one who possesses Merlin's gifts obtained them he knows not whence. Nor does he know what he has, or why he has it, or what it means. So he has questions. Of course he does, he must. So he seeks Merlin. Because he seeks answers. And I am one who has answers. I have things I could tell you. For I am one who has long existed, one who has seen many things and talked with many creatures. I know things which I think you would wish to know. Things, perhaps, about *dragons*?"

It paused and watched Geo's reaction as it said the word *dragons*.

"Yes," it continued, "I think I have not missed the mark. There is much I could teach you about dragons."

Then it looked away, across the forest.

"But," it said, "I am hungry, and I tire, and the day wanes. I must be away to my treasure place. If you would see my treasure, if you would learn what I can teach, if you would receive such gifts as I have to give, then come. If not, then fare well wherever you may go."

Then the thing turned its back on Geo and began lumbering across the clearing away from him.

Geo hesitated, watching the creature lurch away in its long, uneven strides.

What does it know? Geo wondered. *What can it tell me? And how will I ever find out if I don't follow it now?*

Geo began walking after it.

Mont Saint-Michel, the island off the coast of France where King Arthur fought and killed the monster which would not reveal its name

Chapter 23

Where Your Treasure Is, There Will Your Heart Be

From Alette's research notes:

> *Grendel was once of humankind, but over the long ages he had become twisted into were-form, huge, with taloned hands. At night he crept forth from the mere where he dwelt and went in search of prey, always with a marvelously wrought pouch fastened about him. At all times he kept the pouch on his person. It was beautiful. How, in the devious ways of his miserable existence, he had come to possess it was something even the skalds of the most ancient days never knew.*

See *Beowulf* (circa 700 A.D.)

Geo followed after the creature as it shambled through the forest. It was much larger than he was, with longer legs, which made it hard to keep up with, especially in thick undergrowth. As a result the creature stayed always well ahead of him and when Geo tried to ask more questions it only grunted and muttered over its shoulder in its low, growling voice: "Patience. You must have patience. Come see my treasure and from it you will learn much."

The creature led Geo toward higher ground and as the sun began to set they came to a place of rocky hills. The thing started up the steep slope of one of the hills and Geo struggled after it. As the creature climbed it struck a path winding through the trees and turned onto it, following the path higher.

When Geo reached the path he saw the creature walking on it up ahead of him, climbing uphill. Geo followed. Ahead was a break in the trees where the path let out onto a clearing. The creature entered the clearing ahead of Geo and turned to the side so that Geo lost sight of it behind the screening trees.

Geo continued climbing upward on the path until he came to the edge of the clearing. There he paused to survey what lay ahead.

The clearing was a level space on the side of the hill below a stone outcropping at the hill's summit. The remnants of a firepit, all cold ash and black char now, stood in the middle of the clearing, with bracken and broken branches piled around it in messy heaps. Amid the clutter Geo could make out bits of antler and bone.

Across the clearing, in a sheer face of rock where the stone summit ascended vertically, beside a huge boulder, was the dark opening of a cave.

The creature sat in the center of the clearing on a log by the firepit, waiting for Geo. It pointed across the clearing to the cave entrance.

"In there," it said, "you will find my treasure, what I have to show you."

"What is it?" Geo asked.

"Much. Much have I sought, much have I found. Look for yourself and you will know."

Geo hesitated.

"It is my treasure," said the creature enticingly, "and each person's treasure tells that person's story, for those who know how to read it."

Geo edged around the clearing toward the cave, keeping the creature in his line of sight as he skirted the clearing along the tree line. When he reached the cave entrance he saw it was low and narrow. In the deepening twilight it was too dark to see inside. Geo gathered light into his hand from the evening air and cast a thin, tremulous beam into the interior.

Something glinted within. Geo peered closer. Inside the cave he could make out a heap of small, round objects, perhaps coins. Some were shiny, most dull and moldering.

Geo looked back at the creature. It still sat on the log in the center of the clearing, watching Geo. It motioned to him to enter.

With the light still held in his hand, Geo turned back to the opening, ducked his head, and went in.

Inside the roof of the cave was much higher than the entrance. Geo stood and raised his hand above his head, shining the wan light of the early twilight stars around the shadowy interior. A messy detritus of filth and oddments was scattered about: frayed ends of dingy rope, fragments of bone tramped into the dirt floor, brown leaves and the black remnants of old fires.

And there was the pile of coins. In places an occasional metallic gleam shown through the dust and grime of ages. Geo bent to inspect the pile, wondering what the creature thought it would tell him.

Scooping up a handful of the small, dirt encrusted metal discs, he let them cascade through his fingers to fall back into the pile. Some were perforated, with small, evenly spaced holes punched into them. Others had small metal hoops attached to one side. On one the faint outlines of a design could be made out through its patina of accumulated grit. Geo picked it up and rubbed away grime with his thumb.

Suddenly, with a shock, he realized what they were: not coins, but *buttons*.

It was an enormous pile of buttons.

Geo kicked the pile and a skittering of buttons and buckles and other metal bits left from long ago disintegrated clothing slid down to the cave floor.

Geo heard a scraping at the cave entrance and turned.

The great boulder from beside the mouth of the cave was being pushed across the entrance to seal it closed.

Chapter 24

The Lair of Grendel

From Alette's research notes:

Baldr shown with a bright white light and he had been given a gift so that no weapon could pierce him. He was beautiful, and all who beheld him marveled, except for one: that one with an evil heart who became the father of monsters. That one brooded with dark thoughts and said to himself, "There must be another way to slay him."

See *The Prose Edda* (circa 1200 A.D.)

From Alette's research notes:

Grendel had his lair in a dark mere deep within a swamp and there he kept his treasures. But in his hunger for man-flesh, Grendel crept from his lair and made his way at night to Heorot, Hrothgar's golden hall. There he stood in the darkness outside the hall, hating the light within, hating the laughter, hating the life that abounded in bright Heorot. With the protection he possessed, Grendel feared no blade or sharp point, whether of sword or arrow or spear. He stalked Heorot waiting until late in the night when the fires burned low and the King's thanes slept. Then would he sneak within and snatch a poor soul from the bench where he slept and devour him.

But this night, when Grendel slunk into the hall, there awaited him a warrior of strength and courage named Beowulf. Beowulf had heard that the monster fought bare handed, never using sword or knife or spear, so Beowulf determined that he also would fight bare handed when he faced the monster. Thus Beowulf put his trust not in the cunning or craftsmanship of man, with his ingenious weapons of iron and steel, but in the strength given him by God.

That night, when Grendel crept into the hall, Beowulf was awake and waiting for him. Beowulf seized Grendel, and though Grendel smote and writhed, Beowulf held him fast. Grendel could not break Beowulf's grasp and when he tried to wrench himself free Grendel's whole arm was ripped from its socket.

Bubbling gore spilled out. Grendel fled to his lair and disappeared beneath the waters of the lake and there he died.

Beowulf followed after him and entered into the lair of Grendel. There he found many curious things which Grendel had acquired by theft and murder over his long ages of slinking and violence, and Beowulf returned to Heorot loaded with treasures from Grendel's lair.

But Grendel was only one of his kind. Others still walked the wild places and hated Beowulf and all men.

See *Beowulf* (circa 700 A.D.)

"NO!" Geo roared and rushed toward the entrance. Rage surged within him.

The creature outside laughed a wicked cackle.

"See what you have learned! Now here is my gift to you!" it shrieked. "Patience! Patience while you wait in the dark to die! You can be pierced by hunger! You can be riven by thirst! There is more than one way to slay the bearer of Nimue's Gift!"

Geo's only thought was to get out. The stone must not close on him.

The creature stepped in front of the cave to block the opening as it heaved on the stone.

Geo charged toward the entrance and felt his body changing as he moved. His shoulders thickened, the muscle of his body grew heavy and dense. His voice deepened into a roar.

His mouth extended into a broad snout, he felt massive fangs emerge from his jaw bones. Thick, shaggy fur covered his body.

He had transformed into a Kodiak bear, enormous and strong, and he slammed into the creature where it stood across the cave entrance with all the force of fifteen hundred pounds of sinew and bone and muscle.

The creature staggered from the impact, but did not fall and was not dislodged from its position athwart the mouth of the cave.

It set its feet and shoved back against Geo, screaming, "It is mine! Mine by right!"

It thrust against Geo with its thick legs and Geo felt himself being pushed backwards into the cave.

Geo roared and his legs scrabbled against loose earth and bare stone trying to find purchase to halt his backward slide.

The creature lowered its shoulder and grunted, shoving harder.

Geo opened his great jaws and bit, his fangs striking the flesh where the creature's neck joined its shoulders, sinking deep into muscle and sinew. A gush of hot blood flooded Geo's mouth.

The creature went berserk. Shrieking in shock and terror it clawed at Geo with its taloned fingers and slammed Geo side to side against the stone entryway of the cave, frantic to shake him loose and break the hold of Geo's bite.

Acrid blood pumped into Geo's mouth and throat. He gagged, but did not let go of his bite. Everything in him screamed that he must hold his grip, that the bite of his fangs meant life or death.

The next minutes were some of the worst Geo had ever known. The horrible smell of the creature, its panic and madness as it struggled against the bite of Geo's clenched jaws, the thick blood oozing into Geo's throat, choking him.

The creature smashed and clawed at Geo, trying to break free, but Geo bit harder and harder, driving his fangs deeper through muscle and tendon until he struck bone, and still he bit.

The claws of Geo's hind feet dug into the cave floor, found solid footing, and he pushed forward.

The creature shuddered and staggered back.

Geo's legs shoved harder and now the creature began to give ground, slowly yielding as Geo strove forward.

Inch by agonizing inch, Geo pushed his way out of the cave.

The creature's strength slackened, the force of its frenzied clawing and gouging lessened. It convulsed in a spasm.

With a final, great heave Geo shoved the creature backward and drove out of the cave and into the night.

The creature buckled and crumpled to the ground under the force of Geo's drive.

Geo stood atop the fallen creature, still holding his death grip, still biting with all his might. The creature's twisted form writhed beneath him. Geo kept the death grip of his fangs until its struggling subsided, its limbs no longer twitched, and blood no longer pumped from its neck into Geo's mouth.

It was dead.

Finally Geo released his bite and staggered back, gasping for air.

The sky above burned red with sunset. Geo, still in the form of an enormous bear, stood on two legs and roared at the flaming heavens, roared in triumph, roared for life, roared until the forest trembled.

He lowered his head and looked at the creature's mangled corpse in the dirt. Blood pooled under its grotesque, wrecked form.

Geo stood panting, his sides heaving. He sucked in the cool air of evening, drawing its cleanness into himself, and felt himself changing again, growing smaller, the thickness of his shoulders receding as he returned to his own shape.

When he was fully restored to his own form, he began to examine himself to see what injuries the creature had inflicted on him in the madness of its death throws.

Unbelievably, Geo was not even scratched.

He hadn't realized how thick and tough the hide of a bear must be.

Geo looked at the disgusting corpse.

What was it? he wondered. *Where did it come from? What was its name?*

Night was settling over the clearing. Geo walked back to the cave. It was almost full dark now, but he gathered a sliver of starlight and shined it into the dark interior. Within, the gruesome hoard sparkled in the ray of silvery light.

And who were they? Geo wondered.

He let the starlight fade from his hand. He transformed again into the gigantic bear and pushed the stone across the cave entrance, sealing it.

Let this be their tomb, he thought, *whoever they were.*

Geo turned and strode past the corpse of the creature without looking at it.

The insects can take it, he thought, *if they'll have it.*

In the form of a massive bear Geo left the tomb and started down the hill through the dark night.

The Newport Tower located in Newport, Rhode Island, is a stone tower of unknown origin found by early European colonists to America. An armored skeleton was unearthed nearby and placed in a local museum, where it was lost in a fire in 1843. Before the skeleton and its armor were destroyed Henry Wadsworth Longfellow viewed them and wrote the poem "The Skeleton in Armor" about the tower and skeleton. The Westford Knight, an ancient carving of a knight cut into a stone, and the Narragansett Rune Stone, were also discovered in the same area and are now, like The Newport Tower, on public display

Chapter 25

What We Relinquish, What We Retain

From Alette's research notes:

Arthur was sorely wounded in his final battle with Mordred, even to the point of death, and looked upon the great field of carnage. Of all the great hosts that met in bloody battle that day, only two knights remained: King Arthur himself, and his knight Bedevere.

"Lord have mercy," said Arthur as he surveyed the desolation. "All my good knights, all my good knights, take pity on their souls, Dear Lord."

King Arthur could no longer stand upon his feet, so Bedevere carried him to a small chapel by the lake near Salisbury plain wherein was the Island of Avalon.

"Robbers descend on the field of battle to scavenge from the noble knights lying dead or dying," Bedevere told King Arthur. "It would be best if you were brought to some fortified place with high walls."

"No," said Arthur, "I feel the chill of death, it draws near. There is no time to waste, take Caliburn and throw it into the lake."

Bedevere was aghast and hesitated, thinking what

a terrible thing it would be to cast the great Caliburn into the waves.

"I command you!" said Arthur. "Cast Caliburn into the water! Do not delay! You imperil my life every moment you hesitate! I will kill you myself if you do not cast Caliburn into the water!"

So Bedevere took the famous sword and brought it to the edge of the water and with all his might cast it out into the deep. And wonder! When the sword had been cast into the water a boat came gliding out of the mist with lighted lanterns at its sides. Many good and beautiful maidens and married or widowed dames, even princesses and queens, were on the vessel, all in rich array, and among them as their chief was Nimue, The Lady of the Lake. They came and took Arthur and placed him on the ship and went back out again onto the lake.

As the boat disappeared into the mist Sir Bedevere cried out: "Sire! What shall we do without you!"

"I go to Avalon to be healed of my wounds," Arthur called back. "From there I will come again when the hour of most desperate need falls on the folk. Until then, you shall see me no more. But whether or not you receive tidings of me after this, petition God on my behalf, that He help me, strengthen me, and have mercy on me."

See *Le Morte D'Arthur*, Sir Thomas Malory (circa 1450 A.D.); see *Roman de Brut*, by Wace (circa 1150 A.D.); see *Brut*, by Layamon (circa 1190 A.D.)

Geo trundled through the forest in the form of a bear until he came to a swift flowing stream. There he plunged into the water to wash away all stain of the creature. When he emerged again from the water he transformed to ride the wind and swept up into the sky.

He flew through the night to the restless waters of Superior, shimmering with the light of the moon and stars, and followed the great lake's curving shore. He felt a tremendous urgency to reach Alette. Flying as fast as the winds could carry him, he traced the course of the coast around the lake toward the rocky cove where he knew there was a trail that led to an old cabin hidden in the great northern forest where he would find Alette.

He flew on and on, not caring how the wind cut into him, only that he reach her.

When sunrise broke over the rim of the world the waters of Superior shown golden in the day's first light. And then he saw it: the cove, and there, moored within, *The Morning Star*.

He spotted the path through the trees and followed it from the air, flying until he came to the clearing with the cabin.

And there she was, outside in the clearing, in front of the cabin bending over an open fire, cooking.

Geo swept overhead and as the wind rushed over her Alette stood and looked at the sky. Her eyes found him and she stared.

Geo circled, descending on a spiral of wind until he reached the ground and stepped out of the swirling gust to materialize before her.

She ran to him and threw her arms around him.

Tears streamed down her face. With her head against his chest she stood, holding him and crying. Geo wrapped his arms around her and bent his head to press his cheek against her shining, golden hair.

They stood a long time, locked together, holding each other.

"Alette," Geo said at last and she turned her face up to look into his eyes.

"Geo," she said, "you don't know how I've worried, how I've prayed, how I've longed for you to come."

Geo told her, "I have wanted to see you so badly it hurt."

They kissed.

Chapter 26

And Now To See

From Alette's research notes:

> *"Now watch and learn,"* said Merlin, *"that knowledge is more powerful than brawn."*

See *Roman de Brute*, by Wace (circa 1150 A.D.); see *The History of the Kings of Britain*, by Geoffrey of Monmouth (circa 1130 A.D.)

Geo and Alette sat by the fire talking and eating. Geo told her all he had done, the places he had been, and what he had heard from the dragons. He told her about his encounter with the creature.

Alette listened, then told Geo what she'd discovered poring over ancient chronicles while she waited and worried and prayed. She'd recorded all her finding in her research journal.

Geo was amazed at the things she'd found. He was glad to have her on his side. He might not have Merlin to ask his questions to, but with Alette, he might not need him.

He smiled as Alette described the organization of her research program. It was so like her: systematic, logical, reasoned, persistent, tireless. That was how she worked, piecing together different fragments, looking for patterns, never stopping until she found the answer.

"Wait until you go through all the *Cycles* in *The Book of Merlin*," Geo told her, "you'll learn so much from them. Besides, you'll need them. But not now. We can't open the book now. The power that flows from the book when it's opened draws the dragons to it."

They talked until morning had passed into afternoon, then Alette led Geo into the cabin to show him her research journal. Inside, the cabin was just as Geo remembered it: the one table in the middle of the main room, the great fieldstone fireplace, the wide bench along the wall where he had slept the summer before, and the loft up above that served as Alette's room.

Alette's research journal was on the table with books piled around it. Geo sat down, opened the journal, and began to read Alette's notes.

It was fascinating. He recognized names and phrases he had heard from the dragons. And the descriptions of Merlin and Arthur and the powers they wielded against the dragon-men were like echoes from the nights and days he had just been through. He read page after page, losing himself in the history of Arthur and Merlin and Nimue.

And as he read, something tugged at a thread somewhere in the tangled jumble of his thoughts. There was something here, he could sense it, something he needed to know. But what it was he could not grasp. He felt as if he was looking right through it, as if it was somewhere here before his eyes but his exhausted mind could not recognize it and catch hold of it hidden amid the welter of details.

At some point Alette lit an oil lamp and put it on the table. Geo was so absorbed in the research journal he didn't notice. He read the entire journal, then went back and began re-reading passages that seemed to get closer to whatever it was that niggled at his mind.

Alette put a hand on his shoulder and Geo looked up. He was surprised to see it was dark outside.

"I made dinner," Alette said. "We better eat and then you need sleep."

"I'm sorry!" Geo said. "I didn't realize it was getting so late! Thank you for making dinner."

They went out under the stars and ate beside the campfire. After dinner they cleaned-up and went back into the cabin for the night.

Alette had arranged cushions and blankets on the wide bench in the main room for Geo to sleep on as he had last summer.

"I am so glad you're here," she said, hugging him goodnight. "This will be the first night since that morning at Copper Harbor that I'll really sleep. Tonight my prayers will be prayers of thanksgiving."

"Mine too," Geo told her, and they kissed.

"Goodnight," he said, "I love you."

"I love you," she answered and climbed the ladder to the loft above.

Geo settled himself on the bench, pulled the warm

blankets over him, and fell asleep thinking of King Arthur, and a serpent in a field, and a boat from Avalon gliding over misty waters.

* * *

Geo woke the next morning to the smell of sausages frying over the campfire outside. Alette was already up and cooking. When Geo came out she was scrambling eggs in her father's old Dutch oven. Potatoes fried along with the sausages in another pan and coffee percolated in a tin pot set on the coals.

It smelled heavenly.

He sat down on a log near the fire, felt the cool of the morning, the warmth of the fire, heard the sizzle in the pan and smelled the brewing coffee. And there was Alette.

"Thank you," he told her.

"I love you," she answered. "I'm glad when I can do something for you."

She looked at him and the expression in her beautiful eyes filled Geo in a way he had never experienced before. He reached out his hand to touch hers.

They sat there in silence holding hands, looking into each other's eyes.

Suddenly Geo gave a start. He knew. It came to him in an instant. What he had sensed as he read the research journal yesterday, what he had felt he was seeing without recognizing, had just broken through.

Like the tumblers in a lock turning until they

clicked, the thoughts revolving in the back of his mind had finally aligned under Alette's turning of the key and now he understood.

"That's it," he said. "Nimue's Gift."

Geo let go of Alette's hand, stood, and walked back to the cabin.

"What's it?" Alette asked. "What about Nimue's Gift?"

Geo didn't answer. What he had thought he knew about Nimue's Gift had just shifted, and now he knew what he had to do. First, though, he wanted to check his new understanding against Alette's research.

He went into the cabin, sat down at the table, and began looking through the journal, rereading key texts.

Alette entered the cabin behind him. Geo didn't look up, he was too intent on finding those passages that now fit together like pieces of a puzzle.

One after another, they fell into place. It was all here. It had been the whole time, he just hadn't seen it.

"What are you looking for?" Alette asked.

Geo was silent. He knew what he had to do, but he didn't yet see how to do it, at least not without Alette trying to follow him. And she would, whether he wanted her to or not. Once she understood she would not let him go alone. And he knew that she would understand soon. She would put it together faster than he had and he must be away before she did. But she also had to know, for her own safety. But not now, not yet.

"What is it?" Alette asked. "What did you figure out?"

Geo took a moment to think before he answered, searching for the words that would, in time, reveal the truth, but wouldn't give away too much too soon.

He turned to her and asked, "Why would Merlin give Nimue his book, if Nimue already made her own book of all he had taught her?"

"Maybe Merlin's book had other things he hadn't shown her before?" Alette suggested.

"Maybe," Geo said. "But why would the dragons want *The Book of Merlin*?"

"For the power it gives," she answered.

"But the book only allows certain things to be read, as it chooses," Geo said. "That's why we could never read ahead or go back. Do you think the Spartoi could read anything in it?"

"Maybe they want to destroy it," Alette said, "so no one else can gain its power?"

Geo nodded his head in agreement. "That would make sense," he agreed, "but there's something more. The creature in the forest, the Grendel," Geo pointed to the extract about Grendel in Alette's research journal, "it didn't seek to destroy. It sought to possess. It intended to seal me in the cave and take Nimue's Gift from my dead corpse after I starved to death. *There are other ways to destroy the bearer of Nimue's Gift,*' it said."

Alette was silent, thinking.

Geo stood. He hoped he hadn't said too much. It was time to go.

He turned and strode out into the clearing.

Alette ran after him.

"What are you doing?" she cried.

Geo stopped in the clearing and turned to face her.

She came up to him and put her hands on his shoulders.

"You're going, aren't you? To fight them?" Alette said. "I'm coming with you."

"I knew you'd say that," Geo said, "but you can't. You have to live."

"I have to live!" Alette shouted. "Does that mean you think you won't!"

"Alette," Geo said, "take this," and Geo lifted the strap of the golden case off over his head and placed it over Alette's so it hung from her shoulder across her chest.

"I'll follow you!" Alette told him.

"You can't," Geo said. "You haven't gone through the *Cycle* for entering the wind."

"As soon as you leave, I'll go through every *Cycle* in Merlin's damned book! I'll bring the dragons here myself!" she said.

"Alette," Geo said, and she looked into his eyes.

Geo bent and kissed her.

They kissed long, then Geo pulled away from her.

"I love you," he told her.

"I love you, and I won't let you do this!" she said.

"I love you, and that's why I must," said Geo. "Just consider this: what if Nimue's Gift isn't what she received, but what she gave? I give it to you."

"Where are you going?" Alette demanded.

"I'm following where King Arthur went," Geo said and he stepped back, dissolved into the wind, and

173

swirled away into the sky.

He watched Alette on the ground below as he spiraled upward. She stood in the morning light, beautiful, so beautiful. The golden case slung over her shoulder gleamed in the sunshine. Nimue's Gift.

But it no longer contained *The Book of Merlin*. That Geo held in his hand. He had slipped it from the golden case as he kissed her, before stepping back. He knew that if she had the book she would use it.

He wanted her to have it, but not until it was all over. And he needed it to lure the dragons to himself, and away from Alette, away from Nimue's Gift.

* * *

In the clearing Alette saw Geo fade into the sparkling, ethereal form of air and sky, felt the rush of wind, and then he was gone, whisking away.

Hot tears stung her eyes.

She was going after him, right now.

She would activate *The Second Cycle* from *The Book of Merlin* and follow him. She grasped the golden case, felt the tingle of power in her fingertips, and opened it.

The case was empty.

She looked again.

She still felt the charge of power in her fingers, but *The Book of Merlin* was not there.

And then she knew.

She understood.

And she knew that Geo knew. That's what he meant

when he said, "That's it. Nimue's Gift."

That's why he gave it to her.

She wept. She wept with love, with rage, with frustration. Most of all she wept for him, that wonderful, terrible, beautiful man.

The Royal Mounds of Gamla Uppsala, Sweden, barrows of kings named in the Beowulf saga

Gudrun Arms Her Sons With the Treasure of Fafnir

From Alette's research notes:

Princess Gudrun had been married to Sigurd, who slew the dragon Fafnir and took Fafnir's treasure. After Sigurd was murdered, Fafnir's treasure passed into Gudrun's keeping.

Sigurd and Princess Gudrun had a daughter together who was called Svanhild. She, like her father Sigurd, met a cruel fate. Svanhild was murdered by the powerful king Jormunrek.

After Princess Gudrun learned that Jormunrek had murdered Svanhild, she went to her sons Hamdir and Sorli and said to them: "Go, kill King Jormunrek in his hall."

Jormunrek had thanes by the tens and hundreds seated on the benches of his great hall.

Nevertheless, Gudrun's sons were willing, provided Gudrun would first arm them from the treasures of Fafnir.

"We will do as you bid us, Mother," answered Hamdir, "but if you would send us two alone against the horde of Jormunrek you must equip us with the things you keep hidden."

Gudrun was filled with glee, glad her sons would take their swords to make a banquet feast for the crows in Jormunrek's high hall, and she agreed to give them the things they desired from the treasures of Fafnir. She ran to get them from where they were kept hidden and gave them to her sons.

When she had bestowed them on her sons they rode forth, grim and fierce, to Jormunrek's hall.

Jormunrek's watchmen saw them coming and ran to tell Jormunrek.

When Jormunrek heard that the two sons of Gudrun were riding together to his hall, he looked around at his benches full of thanes and laughed, and all his thanes laughed with him.

"Let them come!" King Jormunrek jeered. "What can two alone do against so many? I call it good fortune when my enemy's sons ride to my door! I shall give them the same welcome I gave their sister Svanhild!"

But an old woman in their midst spoke up with a word of warning. "What can it mean," she asked, "if the sons of Gudrun, the Keeper of Fafnir's Treasure, come riding so bold to your hall?"

No one paid her any heed.

They soon learned better! The sons of Gudrun made that hall shake with war! Red ran the blood and drenched all the king's glittering hall as the brothers, relentless, fought their way through rank after rank of thanes, piling corpses on either side of them as they hewed a path to Jormunrek, all the while remaining unscathed themselves.

The brothers broke through at last to Jormunrek and hacked him to pieces. Then, as he lay dying, Jormunrek looked up and saw, and understood, and cried out, "Throw away your weapons my thanes! Keen edges and sharp points will not bite their flesh, these sons of Gudrun!"

Now it was Hamdir who laughed and said, "So now you see! Indeed it must be your lucky day Jormunrek, for happy is the man who perceives and understands! Yet happier still would be the man who perceived and understood sooner!"

See *The Poetic Edda* (circa 900 A.D.)

Drawing of The Ramsund Carving located near Ramsund, Sweden, depicting Sigurd slaying the dragon Fafnir

Chapter 27

Finding Avalon

I walked in that lost wilderness, in the dark of night, far from the farthest outposts of civilization, and there I heard a strange music, as of a great, deep voice singing a haunting melody such as I had never heard before. I could not stop myself from following it, to see what this wild, eerie music might be. And there, in a clearing under the moonlight, stood an enormous bear. There was a hollow tree in the clearing and the bear thrummed the branches of the tree so that the tree vibrated and from its hollow trunk throbbed a low, unworldly tone. While the bear struck these strange tones from the tree it raised its head to the moon and stars and sang. What its song portended, I could not say, but it haunts my memory still, like a specter of the wild.

See *The Long Walk*, by Slavomir Rawicz (1956)

There are over four hundred islands scattered throughout Lake Superior. Many have never been named, or if they were once named, it was by civilizations long since vanished, and their names disappeared with them.

Only a few of those hundreds of islands are inhabited, and of those most only seasonally. Just a handful have year-round residents. The far reaches of Superior are simply too remote from the current centers of human society for people to live there, so its distant islands have become, in our time, an isolated and unknown wilderness.

There have been more shipwrecks in the Great Lakes than in the Bermuda Triangle. Storms whip up suddenly on Superior and can be utterly ferocious, with crushing forty-foot waves. Its deep, cold waters are powerful and unforgiving.

That remoteness and inaccessibility were exactly what Geo wanted now, so that no one else would be caught up in what he was about to do. And he didn't want Alette finding him, not yet. He knew it wouldn't take her long to decipher the riddle he'd left her. Which was good. If, when it was all over, he wasn't able to give her *The Book of Merlin* himself, she'd find it when she found Avalon, wherever that might turn out to be.

That she would find Avalon Geo had no doubt. He knew Alette wouldn't give up until she did.

And he would help her. He would leave her a sign.

Hopefully she'd never need the sign. Geo still intended to give her *The Book of Merlin* with his own hands. He was prepared to die if he must, but he didn't want to. He wanted to make the dragons die.

And he had an idea of how to do it. Now he just needed the place.

So he swept through the air, riding the wind high above the sparkling waters of Superior, searching. The northeast coast of Superior from Marathon to Wawa is a vast, undeveloped wilderness with no towns, no villages, no highways. And all along that coast are innumerable islands, beautiful, mostly rocky, many with high, steep cliffs, and covered with fragrant pine. On one of those islands he could isolate the danger he intended to create.

So he flew on from island to island, exploring and reconnoitering. He knew the islands would be devoid of people. That was a given. But he didn't want other creatures hurt in the coming storm either. Caribou and moose lived on some islands of Superior, having swum, or walked across the ice when the lake was frozen, to find new homes. Predators had followed, so wolves, cougars, lynx, bobcats, and bear could all be found on various islands, along with many other smaller animals.

Geo also needed a place to hide *The Book of Merlin* where it would be safe until Alette could find it, and his Avalon needed a good landing place for her to come ashore from *The Morning Star*.

So he searched, riding the wind down the lonely, beautiful coast. And then, as the sun began to set, he finally found it: a medium sized island, forested, lying a few hundred yards from shore, with steep sides of rock ascending to a high, jagged peak in its center. From the base of a great cliff of weathered granite, a beach of smooth, rounded stones sloped down to the water. The stones were of many colors and many sizes, some large and some small. Two enormous, dome-shaped boulders stood like sentinels, one on each end the beach. It was a perfect landing place for Alette.

The island was maybe eighty yards long and, at its widest, fifty yards across.

It was what he needed.

Geo swung down on a current of wind and materialized out of the air onto the stony beach.

Looking around, he was struck by what an amazing place it was. The waters of Lake Superior were quiet in the deepening twilight. Waves gently lapped the stones of the beach with a soft, rhythmic whooshing. Atop the cliffs, wind whistled in the pines. It was like paradise.

He sat down on the rocky beach and looked at the sky. Not much daylight remained, and he would need the light to see the dragons approaching. He would have to wait until tomorrow.

Geo transformed into a bear so he would have its thick fur to keep him warm through the night. He found a place sheltered from the wind at the back of the beach, against the cliff, and lay down to sleep.

But sleep would not come.

He watched the moon rise and thought about tomorrow, what it would hold. He thought of Alette. And something from within the nature of a bear, from deep within the ursine bones that were now bound to his soul, made him raise his face to the moon and sing a song he did not understand.

Chapter 28

Come Dragons, Come

From Alette's research notes:

Morgan Le Fay hated her brother Arthur, not because of anything Arthur had ever done, but because he was good and she was evil, and evil always and everywhere hates good, without reason, without remorse.

Morgan plotted to kill Arthur, but knew that first she must steal his scabbard, or no sword would cut him, no arrow pierce him. For Morgan was skilled in many arts and knew many things, all of which she turned to evil, much to the sorrow of all the land, and she knew what the scabbard truly was.

So while Arthur slept, she crept into his room and stole the scabbard from his side, for Arthur kept it always with him, even in his sleep.

Arthur felt its absence. He woke, saw that the scabbard was gone, and asked who had been in his chamber. Attendants told him that his sister, Morgan Le Fay, had come in while he slept.

"My horse!" Arthur cried. He armed himself with Caliburn and set out after her immediately.

Morgan rode ahead of him with a retinue of twenty knights. When she and her men-at-arms looked back and saw King Arthur riding so hard and coming so fast, they knew he would overtake them, and they trembled, for Arthur was mighty, and though they were many they feared him greatly.

In desperation, Morgan looked around. She was by the side of a mere.

"If I cannot have the scabbard," she said, "at least <u>he</u> *will not!"*

And so declaring, she flung the scabbard into the lake.

Thus it was that when Arthur came to face Mordred, who was Morgan Le Fay's son and who, together with Arthur's wife Queen Guenevere, had stolen Arthur's throne in his absence, then Arthur had it not.

See *Le Morte D'Arthur*, by Sir Thomas Malory (circa 1450 A.D.); see *The Merlin Continuation* of the Post-Vulgate Cycle, by Anonymous (circa 1235 A.D.)

Geo woke in the morning to find mist brooding over Lake Superior, wreathing the surface of the water and shrouding the island.

Good, Geo thought, *the mist will help.*

He rose, shook out his fur, and transformed back into human shape. He searched for a place to hide Merlin's book and found a deep fissure high up in the stone face of the cliff which backed the rocky beach. There *The Book of Merlin* would be safe until Alette could find it, out of reach of the waves below and sheltered above from the rain and snow.

He did not place the book in the crevice yet. He still needed it to call the dragons. But he knew he would have to act quickly once he had summoned them, so he wanted the hiding place picked-out and prepared in advance.

Next, he set to work building a cairn of stones as a marker and sign to guide Alette. He gathered large stones from the rocky beach and piled them in a pyramid. Then he lashed sticks together in a cross and placed it in the top of the cairn, held upright by the stones.

When this was done he stood and surveyed the island. Waves washed on the shore, wind stirred the pines, and mist flowed over the surface of the water. It was beautiful.

He wondered where Alette was right now.

Geo knelt on the beach before the wooden cross he had made.

"Dear Lord," he prayed, "help Alette, wherever she is. Guide her, guard her, protect her. And help me this day. Let me triumph. Give me victory. Let me live, and let me kill the dragons. Let me see Alette again."

He bowed his head, concentrating on what he had to do, praying for strength, praying for victory.

Then he stood, removed his flannel shirt and laid it out on the stones of the beach, ready to wrap *The Book of Merlin*.

Next Geo summoned winds, gathering great, swirling gusts and weaving them together to wrap around the island, encircling it with a spiraling column of rushing air. The winds drew the fog from the lake into their midst as they spun upward into the sky.

Geo reached out to draw shadow to him, harvesting the dark recesses beneath bough and boulder, and cast it into the wind and mist so that they grew dim and murky, colored with shades of twilight. The resulting pillar of dark, revolving cloud towered into the sky over the island, engulfing it in dense gloom.

If there had been a ship plying those distant waters, its crew would have beheld a strange, ominous sight in that dark column of spinning cloud rising alone from the icy waters of the mighty lake.

Geo wielded the powers that had been given him with reckless abandon. A surge of exhilaration filled him. No wonder Merlin had to be careful about dispensing his gifts. The intoxication of the power almost overwhelmed him as he let it flow free and unchecked through him. He didn't worry about avoiding detection. He wanted the dragons to see, and to come.

He would be ready for them when they did.

It was time to call them.

Geo opened *The Book of Merlin*.

The great torrent of energy rushed out, cascading around him, crackling in the air.

Come dragons, Geo thought. *The chase ends here. And the surprise is that I am the hunter, and really have been all along.*

Geo let the power pour out from the book.

When he felt it was time, he closed *The Book of*

Merlin and moved quickly, bundling the book and hiding it in the cleft of the rock. He transformed into the great white bird, spread his wings, and flung himself into the spiraling maelstrom he had created around the island. He climbed through the air within the pillar of dark, spinning cloud. Near its top, but still hidden within its concealing mist, he circled, looking out, searching the sky all around.

Come dragons, he thought, *come.*

Stone ruins along the shores of Lake Superior in Pukaskwa National Park, Ontario, Canada, one of many found on the islands and coasts of Lake Superior

Chapter 29

Where Waves Lap the Shores of Avalon

From Alette's research notes:

It was God Who created justice and peace, and He placed them within the blade of the sword.

See *The Story of Merlin*, by Anonymous (circa 1215 A.D.)

From Alette's research notes:

Arthur received the scabbard at the same time he received Caliburn. Merlin asked him, "Which do you value more?"

Arthur looked at both with wonder, but his eyes sparkled as he beheld the mighty Caliburn.

"Surely the sword," said Arthur.

"That shows," answered Merlin, "that you do not understand the scabbard."

See *Le Morte D'Arthur*, by Sir Thomas Malory (circa 1450 A.D.)

Geo circled within the revolving column of shadowy cloud, peering out. This time it would be he, not the dragons, who would spring the trap.

A black speck appeared in the sky, flying low above the surface of Superior. Geo continued scanning the horizon and saw another dark form coming high in the sky from the opposite side of the island.

They were approaching from different points, as they had done before, trying to take him by surprise. Where would the other two appear?

Just so they entered the mist, Geo thought.

Within the dark, swirling cloud he could isolate the dragons and attack them one at a time rather than having to fight all at once.

Geo saw a third dragon coming, flying over the forest toward the island from yet another point. Only one remained to be accounted for.

The first dragon reached the island and shot a jet of flame into the mist, then entered the churning cloud after it, following the path of his own fire into the darkness within.

Geo lost sight of it in the swirling cloud but a trail of rippling vapors below him marked the dragon's hidden passage through the mists.

Geo looked back out over the lake, searching the sky for the last dragon. The other two still circled outside the column of cloud, peering inward. There was no sign of the fourth dragon. Had the dragons fought? Was the last dragon already dead?

One of the two circling outside the pillar of cloud folded its wings and dove into the heart of the spinning mist, trailing whisps of vapor like tendrils of smoke in its wake as it streaked down toward the island.

There was a heavy thud and the sound of scattering stones as the dragon crashed into the rocky beach below. Then a voice called up from the island through the dark fog: "George Northrup!"

It was Kaya, and it followed its naming of Geo with a wicked laugh.

"Yes, George Northrup," Kaya yelled, "we know who you are! Or should I call you *Geo*? That is what your friends call you, is it not? Come, let us be friends. We shall call you Geo as well."

Geo couldn't see Kaya on the beach below and now he'd lost sight of the dragon he knew still flew hunting for him somewhere within the tower of swirling cloud. He was losing control of the situation.

The third continued circling outside, waiting for a sign of Geo to pounce.

"And where is your pretty friend?" Kaya asked. "What is her name? Oh yes, *Margaret Martel*. But we shall become better acquainted with her as well, so let us call her *Alette*, as you do."

Kaya laughed hideously.

A billow of flame flashed through the air amid the dark clouds, thirty feet below Geo. He looked and saw a head emerging within the vapor beneath him.

He couldn't wait any longer. He had to attack, while

he still knew where the dragons were and before one of them found him and they all converged on him at once.

Geo extended his talons and dove at the dragon in the clouds below him.

He flashed through the sky with blinding speed and struck the dragon like a bolt of lightning, smashing into its head and knocking it out of its flight, the force of the impact jolting its head sideways and sending it careening with flailing wings.

Geo's talons latched onto the dragon at its head and neck, piercing through scaly flesh, ripping and tearing, gouging muscle and veins. With his sharp beak he lashed out at the dragon's face.

He struck an eye and blood spurted from it as it was punctured. The dragon screamed in anguish. Blinded and bleeding, it cartwheeled through the air like a crashing kite, spinning toward the ground.

Geo continued cutting and slashing with his beak and rending with his talons, tearing out hunks of flesh even as the dragon fell from the sky. Geo felt the dragon's muscles spasm in the grip of his talons and it began to transform back into a man as it plummeted through the sky.

Geo released the Spartoi and it crashed in its human form into the trees below. Geo beat his wings to check his own downward descent and landed on the plateau of the cliff top, transforming into his own shape as he touched the rocky summit. He ran toward the grove of trees growing atop the cliff where he'd seen the Spartoi fall.

There, amid broken branches, lay the twisted

corpse where it had crashed through the trees. The Spartoi was dead.

Air rushed behind him and Geo heard a roar. He spun around to see a blazing jet of fire streaking toward him. He dove aside, rolled on the ground, and came up already transformed into ethereal form of sky and air and reached out his hands to gather wind. He swung a shaking typhoon blast to pound into the oncoming dragon as it flew at him through the sky. The wind crashed into the dragon like a hammer blow, smashing it out of the sky and driving it down into one of the great boulders standing guard at the side of the beach. The dragon's back struck against the stone with a sickening snap. It shrieked once, then fell limply back, bent backwards at a sharp angle across the boulder.

Geo barely had time to register the death of the second dragon when he heard Kaya's excited cackle behind him. He turned to see the dragon's head emerging over the rim of the cliff as Kaya clambered up the rock face of the cliff from the beach below.

Geo charged, materializing out of the wind into the form of a massive bear as he ran straight at the dragon. Kaya's shoulders had just cleared the edge of the cliff when Geo slammed full speed into the dragon's chest with all the weight and power of the Kodiak.

Kaya reeled from the impact and was thrown backward to fall from the cliff. Geo tumbled after him, carried over the edge by his own momentum.

The dragon lashed out in mid-air with its claws and tail as it fell. Geo transformed again into the wind and caught an updraft that lifted him out of the dragon's reach.

The dragon hit the beach, sending a shower of stones flying in all directions. Geo transformed into the white bird and dove at Kaya, striking the dragon in the neck, ripping into muscle and sinew. Blood gushed out and Kaya writhed madly. It whipped its head to fling Geo from its neck, sending Geo flying across the beach to slam into the cliff.

Geo smashed into the sheer rock face and fell to the stony beach, transforming back into a man as he crashed down. He tried to rise, but could not. He looked up to see Kaya swaying on his feet, trying stay upright. The dragon's body convulsed in violent spasms as its life blood pumped out of a gaping wound in its neck.

It stumbled and fell. There was a horrible, rasping death rattle, and then the dragon was still.

Geo struggled to his feet, battered and shaky. Cuts burned along his back and legs where sharp edges of stone had ripped through his shirt and pants into his flesh when he was smashed against the cliff.

Before he could steady himself a huge black form exploded from the water and barreled onto the beach straight at him. A taloned claw reached out and lanced him through the abdomen as the dragon drove into him and shoved him backwards again into the cliff, pinning him against its rock face with its long talon piercing through his stomach.

Geo looked down and saw blood welling around the impaling talon. The dragon twisted its claw and Geo was wracked with agony.

Hot breath in his face suffocated him and Geo looked up into the leering smile of Gibber.

"So now," Gibber smirked, "he bleeds."

The dragon threw its head back and roared.

It looked at Kaya's body, then at the carcass of the dead dragon flung across the boulder, and back to Geo.

"It seems, little sparrow," Gibber said, "you have become a bird of prey. I thank you. You have provided me a feast. But a bird of prey would do well to fly with Nimue's Gift under its wing."

Gibber twisted the talon again and white-hot pain lanced through Geo.

"Where is it?" Gibber demanded.

Geo gasped and clutched at his stomach, feeling the blood oozing out.

"Ah, it hurts," Gibber said, twisting the talon again and chuckling as tremors shook Geo.

"It is, I think, a mortal wound," it said. "Unless, that is, one had Nimue's Gift. With Nimue's Gift one might still live. *It* has the power to heal, to save, even now. It can bring a man back from the very edge. It brought Arthur back in Avalon."

The dragon lowered its head so its eyes were level with Geo's.

"Yes," it said, staring into Geo's eyes. "Nimue's Gift was in Avalon. Nimue brought it there. She recovered it from the lake where Morgan threw it. Merlin showed her how to find treasures and retrieve them. It saved Arthur. It can save you. Where is it? Tell me and I will bring it to you."

Geo could not answer. He felt strange, as though

his own body were somehow far away and disconnected from him. Sweat poured from him yet he was chilled and shook uncontrollably.

"You have given me much dust," Gibber said. "We long to consume the dust always, you know. It does not matter to us particularly whether it is from our own or from others, only that we must devour flesh of dust. There is much here already. I thank you for it. I don't need more. Come, tell me where Nimue's Gift is. I will get it and bring it to you. I shall keep it, of course, but as a token of respect for one who has proven a valiant adversary, I will allow it to heal you. Then I will gorge myself on what you have prepared for me."

Geo's eyes lost focus and his vision faded. He was aware that Gibber spoke, but the dragon's voice sounded faint and Geo could not follow the thread of what it was saying. Instead, he began to be aware of other voices, just at the edge of hearing. They seemed to be calling him. He tried to hear what they said, but he could not quite make it out, though it seemed somehow desperately important to know. If only Gibber would be quiet.

"Stay with me," Gibber said. "Don't leave, not yet. Nimue's Gift. Where is it? Gifts are given to be used. Use your gifts, save yourself. Tell me where it is and I will bring it to you."

Through the cold and shadows creeping in around him the dragon's words registered . . . *gifts . . . gifts are meant to be used*.

"Gifts," Geo gasped, his eyes focusing again to see Gibber before him.

"Yes," Gibber encouraged. "Gifts. Use your gifts. Share them. Share them with me."

Geo felt a burning begin within him, deep at his core, a power that swelled and consumed him from within. It would, he realized, take every last particle he had to give. He could not survive it. But then, it was not necessary that he survive it. It was only necessary that he triumph.

Gifts are given to be used.

He had been given a gift.

And it's not done yet, he told himself. *I have to finish it. I must conquer.*

"I will," Geo croaked in a faint whisper, "share my gift."

Gibber's eyes flashed with greed.

"Yes, yes!" he rasped eagerly. "Share it with me!"

The Light of Caliburn burst from Geo, flashing out across Superior. Gibber stood momentarily frozen, shock and horror etched on his face in the white blaze of The Light.

Geo struck downwards with a burning fist, breaking the dragon's leg that pinned him to the cliff. The leg snapped, crunching beneath the blow and folding like a jackknife. The talon slid out of Geo's stomach as the leg bent.

Geo went numb from pain and fell to his knees.

The burning of The Light seared through him.

Kill him! Geo thought. *Now, while you still can!*

He surged back to his feet and swung a burning fist. The blow slammed into Gibber's chest, knocking the dragon sprawling backward onto the stony beach.

Geo rushed at him, but The Light had pulsed onward and now the dragon was free from its hold. From its back it lashed out with its tail, catching Geo on the side and flinging him through the air. Geo crashed into the cairn of stones he had made as a sign for Alette and rocks flew, ricocheting across the beach.

The dragon scrambled to its feet and charged.

Geo rolled and came up on his feet. He grabbed a huge stone from the cairn and ran straight at the charging dragon.

"This is the dust I prepared for you!" Geo screamed and swung the stone in his shining hand.

The blow caught the onrushing dragon on the side of its head, disintegrating its skull on impact.

Brains splattered across the rocky beach and the dragon was thrown sideways, spinning across the beach to land in a heap, dead.

Geo dropped the stone. The Light went out from him. He slumped forward and collapsed onto the beach.

Alette is safe now, he thought.

Then all went black.

Chapter 30

In Avalon

From Alette's research notes:

"Come, and love one who loves you."

See *Le Morte D'Arthur*, by Sir Thomas Malory (circa 1450 A.D.)

From Alette's research notes:

But what one lady cast aside, another gathered in. Out of hatred, Morgan Le Fay threw the scabbard into the lake that none might have it or have life by it. But out of love, another lady recovered it, and gave it to the one she loved, that he might live.

The Merlin Continuation of the Post-Vulgate Cycle, by Anonymous (circa 1235 A.D.)

Geo was aware that he lay against cool stones. He was awake, but did not move.

* * *

Suddenly Geo startled and wondered if he had passed out again.

Or was it the voices?

He thought he heard them again. Yes, they seemed to be growing louder, to be coming nearer. He listened, trying to understand what they said.

He felt terribly cold. He rolled over onto his back and opened his eyes. Sun shone down. The swirling pillar of dark cloud was gone.

His body trembled. He didn't seem to be able to stop its shaking.

He became aware of a stench, a terrible, sick odor of decay. Once he was aware of it, it became overpowering.

He raised his head. A dragon carcass lay before him. It blocked him from the water. He could see nothing else, the stinking dragon corpse filled all his view.

He lay his head down again.

The voices drifted away.

* * *

Geo woke.

He was thirsty; terribly, terribly thirsty.

He wondered if he could reach the water.

The stench of the dragon corpse was oppressive. He wanted to wretch but could not.

He raised his head again, but all he could see was the great bulk of the dead dragon.

No, Geo thought, *not like this. I'm not going to spend my last moments looking at that thing.*

He rolled onto his stomach and began clawing his way over stones, dragging his body across the rocky beach.

He was aware there was pain, but could not really feel it. It was too far away. What troubled him was a clumsiness, an unresponsiveness of his limbs. His body would not seem to do what he wanted it to. But slowly, fumblingly, he made his way around the dragon corpse.

When he cleared it at last he felt the wind off the lake. He looked up and there was Superior, its sparkling blue water stretching away into the distance, shimmering with light.

He crawled on and reached the lake's edge, gulping cool, sweet water as waves lapped against his face.

He pulled himself over to the other great boulder, at the end of the beach across from where the dead dragon lay bent backwards and broken on the other.

He pulled himself into a sitting position, rested his back against the boulder, and looked out on the lake, away from the dead dragons, gazing on water and light.

The wind off Superior drove away the fetid stench of the rotting dragon corpses.

This is good, Geo thought. *Thank you, Jesus, I can go now.*

Geo lay his head back. His vision became fuzzy. He

could not really see the water anymore, only a great blur of light.

He closed his eyes and filled his lungs with the fresh wind. Instead of voices now he heard singing, Alette's singing. She was playing guitar. In his mind he was sitting with her around a campfire.

He smiled.

That is the one thing, Geo thought, *to see Alette again.*

But he knew she was safe now. He had done it. He had won. He had protected her.

Still, to see her face again, Geo thought with a sigh.

He opened his eyes. The light seemed to be growing, coming closer, filling all his vision.

He watched it and wondered, puzzled. He had always heard that people walked toward the light, but this light seemed to be coming to him. Maybe it came because he could not walk anymore.

Then in the midst of the light he saw her: Alette. She was coming to him.

Thank you, Jesus, he thought. *Thank you. It's more than I deserve . . . You didn't have to . . . thank you.*

The vision came to him, burning with Light.

The Light faded and Alette was kneeling beside him.

"Geo, Geo, no Geo, no," he heard her voice sobbing.

He looked up and smiled. He tried to say her name, to speak the word *Alette*, but no sound came.

She saw him move, took his face in her hands. Tears ran down her cheeks and dropped, splashing onto his.

Geo wanted to look on that image, to see her face and hold onto the vision of her as long as he could, to the very end.

Suddenly terrible pain seized him. It spread like fire from his stomach throughout his body. He groaned in agony.

Geo looked down. Against his abdomen, over the dark stain of blood where the talon had pierced him, glittered the golden case.

The intensity of the pain made his body convulse.

"Oh, God," Geo gasped.

All the pain that had seemed distant and disconnected from him now came rushing back, overpowering every nerve of his body.

No, no, it is too much.

He felt Alette's hand smoothing his hair and looked again to her face.

"Live, Geo," she whispered.

His body shook and he whispered, "Alette." This time he heard his voice speak her name aloud.

"Yes," she said, "*your* Alette, Geo. I love you, Geo. I love you. Live Geo, live for me. You fought for me, you would die for me, now live for me. Live, and love one who loves you."

Chapter 31

Children of Idunn

From Alette's research notes:

"I am going away now, and I shall remain hidden. No one shall see me except those I chose to reveal myself to. I shall continue to wage The War, growing young again, regenerating through the ages, until the world comes at last to its end." So saying, Merlin disappeared from their sight and they saw him no more.

See *Perceval*, by Robert de Boron (date unknown, believed circa 1190 A.D.)

From Alette's research notes:

Once Merlin came and when they saw him he was wearing a golden case that hung from a leather strap on his shoulder.

See *The Story of Merlin*, by Anonymous (circa 1215 A.D.)

It was more than a year later. Geo stood before his easel in a mountain meadow of the Keweenaw Peninsula, painting in the golden light of an early autumn evening. Alette sat on a picnic blanket nearby, playing guitar and singing. These days she brought cushions to sit on when they came out after dinner. Her pregnancy was far enough along that it was too uncomfortable for her otherwise. Her baby bump was so pronounced that she had to shift her guitar sideways to play.

Still, they came out together almost every evening, Geo painting and Alette playing and singing and reciting poetry.

Geo was trying to finish as many canvases as he could before the baby came. Recently he found that he worked with a new intensity, painting much more quickly and deftly than he ever did before. And he completed many more canvases than he ever did before.

He also sold more, and for higher prices than he ever commanded before. Which, with the baby on the way, was wonderful.

The paintings themselves had also changed. His art had taken a new direction. He still painted landscapes of the Upper Peninsula, but he had started placing animals in those landscapes as their focal point. He wanted a spark of *life* in each picture he made.

The change had transformed his career. He suddenly found his paintings garnering national, and even international, attention.

What drew the interest of critics and collectors alike was a certain, indefinable quality in the animals. He seemed somehow able to capture the essence of each creature "as if he knew them from the inside," as one critic put it.

Geo was glad for the jump in income that came with his heightened profile. He and Alette had married shortly after returning from the island in Superior. When they left the island they went first to the cabin, and from there to Alette's hometown, where they were married in the same church where Alette's parents had been married. After that they went to the United States embassy to have their marriage civilly recognized across the border. They stayed the rest of the summer at the cabin. Then, with the new school year at Michigan Tech approaching, they returned to the Upper Peninsula, Alette to her teaching and research, and Geo to his easel.

After Geo whisked away on the wind that morning at the cabin Alette had quickly deciphered his reference to Avalon and knew he was going to an island in Superior. She also concluded his probable destination would be somewhere along Superior's northeast coast in the vicinity of Pukaskwa National Park, due to its remoteness.

She immediately set out after him on *The Morning Star*.

When she saw the pillar of dark, swirling cloud the

following day she knew it must be him and sailed toward it. She had gotten near enough to hear the roar of the dragons and the crashings of battle. She saw The Light of Caliburn flash, bright and blinding. Shortly after, the island had become quiet, the winds died down, and the clouds dispersed. She kept scanning the island through her binoculars as she sailed nearer and was almost to the island when she finally spotted him sitting with his back to the giant boulder on the stony beach. That was when she let The Light of Caliburn burn within her and leapt into the water, swimming the rest of the way to him, carrying the golden case with her.

She reached him with the case and it was Nimue's Gift that saved him.

The Light Geo had seen coming to him across the water had been Alette.

And not long after their wedding, they discovered their first child was on the way.

Now they waited for the baby to arrive, painting, singing, and enjoying the autumn evenings of the Upper Peninsula, with the brilliant colors of changing leaves, crisp air, and the warm, golden light. Geo tried to convey the quality of that light in oil on canvas while he listened to Alette's sweet music.

He stepped back now to examine his current picture.

As he did, a magnificent stag emerged from the tree line across the meadow.

Geo paused. There was something arresting about that stag, something familiar.

He quickly wiped his brush clean, dipped it into new pigment, and went to the easel. In a few quick strokes he sketched the stag, trying to capture its majesty.

"That's a fine painting," an old man's voice said behind him and Geo jumped in surprise.

He turned to see an elderly gentleman with a walking stick and the look of one of the Upper Peninsula's many eccentric personalities. Geo must have been concentrating so intently on his painting that he hadn't heard the old man approaching down the trail.

Geo smiled. "Thank you," he said.

Alette smiled also. "He's very talented," she said as she strummed her guitar.

"As are you," the old man answered, turning to her with a smile. "You play beautifully and your voice is exquisite. And *Greensleeves* is my favorite song."

"Thank you," Alette said. "The old folk songs are the best, aren't they?"

"Indeed," the old man agreed, "though I prefer to think of them as *ancient yet ever young*, rather than old."

"I agree," Alette said.

"And that painting," the old man said, turning again to examine Geo's canvas, "is also beautiful. Remarkable how you've portrayed the *heart* of the *hart*, so to speak, with such economy. It's almost as if you could see into the stag's own dreams."

Geo felt an odd tingling along his spine.

"I suppose you must have to work quickly, the way

the light fades," the old man continued.

Geo turned back to the canvas and looked again at the stag in the meadow. Already shadows were lengthening. "Yes," he agreed, "it is a joy to be out here, but it has its challenges."

"As do all things, George," the old man said behind him.

Geo froze. He knew that voice. Where had he heard it?

"That is what I wanted to say to you, why I have come," the old man continued, "to tell you to value what you have been given and tend to it. It will have its challenges, but all things in this world do. The golden case was not Nimue's Gift, it was merely a token of her gift. The real gift which Nimue gave to Pelleas was far greater than the scabbard or any case made from it. It was The Gift, The Gift that Arthur was never given, though Arthur possessed the scabbard. Alas, if only Guenevere had given that Gift to him, I wonder how things might have turned out differently. But you have been given The Gift, just as you have given it. You and Alette have given it to each other. Like the ancient carols sung anew, give it anew each day. Let it be your treasure, always."

Geo spun around, but even as he began to move wind rushed around him and when he looked the old man was gone.

Alette had stopped playing guitar.

She looked at Geo and their eyes met.

Then Alette looked past Geo, over his shoulder, and pointed to the meadow. "Geo! Look!" she said.

Geo turned and saw across the meadow not one, but two glorious stags.

They stood with their heads up, watching Geo and Alette. Then the new stag bowed its head in salute to them, turned, and walked away into the forest. The other stag followed, bowing and then going after it into the woods. Soon they were lost to sight amid the autumn trees.

"Are you going after them?" Alette asked.

Geo slowly shook his head. "No," he said, "I don't think so. Someone once told me that Merlin comes and goes when he will, revealing himself when he chooses, but that he can't be found when he doesn't want to be."

"Do you think we'll ever see him again?" Alette asked.

"I have a feeling," Geo said, "that it's almost certain."

Image Credits

Front cover and front piece on Page 1   The Light of Caliburn, sword, tree, and dragons, original artwork by Jake Frost

Text symbol used throughout: ~~~
Source: Wikimedia Commons; Author: Augusto Castellani (book), Dell'oreficeria ornament7.jpg Carlomorina (scan); Title: typographic ornament of a italian XIX century book; Date: 6 November 2010; License: Creative Commons Attribution-Share Alike 3.0 Unreported; URL: https://commons.wikimedia.org/wiki/File:Dell%27oreficeria_anti ca_ornament7.svg

Page 4   St. Michael's Tower, Glastonbury Tor
Source: Wikimedia Commons; Author: Glastomichelle; Title: Glastonbury Tor; Date: 23 February 2019; License: Creative Commons Attribution-Share Alike 4.0 International; URL: https://commons.wikimedia.org/wiki/File:Daffodils_and_Glasto nbury_Tor.jpg; image modified for publication

Page 8   Dinas Emrys
Source: Wikimedia Commons; Author: James Frankom (talk); Title: ruins of the 11th century tower on Dinas Emrys; Date: 30 December 2008; License: Creative Commons Attribution Share Alike 3.0 Unreported; URL: https://commons.wikimedia.org/wiki/File:Dinas_Emrys_Tower1. jpg; image modified for publication

Page 17   King Arthur
Source: Wikimedia Commons; Author: Sailko; Title: Piazza

Grande (Modena); Date: 4 September 2018; License: Creative
Commons Attribution-Share Alike 4.0 International; URL:
https://commons.wikimedia.org/wiki/File:Ambito_di_wiligelmo,
_porta_della_pescheria,_02_ciclo_di_art%C3%B9_02,2_art%C3
%B9_dei_britanni.jpg; image modified for publication

Page 25   Saint Michael the Archangel from Mont Saint-
Michel
Source: Wikimedia Commons; Public Domain; URL:
https://commons.wikimedia.org/wiki/File:MontStMichel-
StatueFremiet.jpg; image modified for publication

Page 60   Pillar of Eliseg
Source: Wikimedia Commons; Author: Wolfgang Sauber; Title:
Llangollen (Wales) Eliseg's pillar; Date: 14 July 2011; License:
Creative Commons Attribution Share Alike 3.0 Unreported, 2.5
Generic, 2.0 Generic, and 1.0 Generic; URL:
https://commons.wikimedia.org/wiki/File:Elisegs_Pfeiler_4_Nor
den.jpg; image modified for publication

Page 81   Dragon bones on display at The Church of Santa
Maria and San Donato
Source: Wikimedia Commons; Author: Sailko; Title: Santa Maria
and San Donato (Murano)-Interior; Date: 9 August 2018; License:
Creative Commons Attribution 3.0 Unreported; URL:
https://commons.wikimedia.org/wiki/File:Murano,_santi_maria
_e_donato_(duomo),_interno,_assunta_in_stucco_del_xviii_sec
olo_02.jpg; image modified for publication

Page 90   Hammer of Thor
Source: Wikimedia Commons; Author: Lkovac; Title: Hammer of

Thor monument on norther shores of Payne River, Ungava Peninsula, Nunavik, Quebec, Canada; Date: 26 July 2010; License: Creative Commons Attribution-Share Alike 3.0 Unreported; URL: https://commons.wikimedia.org/wiki/File:Hammer_of_Thor_(m onument).jpg; image modified for publication

Page 94   Cliffs along the coast of Lake Superior
Source: Wikimedia Commons; Author: Coates4; Title: Sleeping Giant Provincial Park lookout located in Thunder Bay, Ontario; Date: 28 May 2018; License: Creative Commons Attribution-Share Alike 4.0 International; URL: https://en.wikipedia.org/wiki/File:Sleeping_Giant_Provincial_Pa rk.jpg; image modified for publication

Page 119   Agawa Rock Pictograph
Source: Wikimedia Commons; Author: D. Gorden E. Robertson; Title: Canoe (top left), Michipeshu (top right), and two giant serpents (chignebikoogs), panel VIII, Agawa Rock, Lake Superior Provincial Park, Ontario, Canada; Date: 26 July 2011; License: Creative Commons Attribution-Share Alike 3.0 Unreported; URL: https://commons.wikimedia.org/wiki/File:Agawa_Rock,_panel_ VIII.jpg; image modified for publication

Page 132   Manana Island
Source: Wikimedia Commons; Author: Halfblue; Title: The Town of Monhegan on Monhegan Island, Maine; Date: 2 September 2005; License: Creative Commons Attribution-Share Alike 3.0 Unreported; URL: https://commons.wikimedia.org/wiki/File:Monhegan_pano.jpg; image modified for publication

Page 146   Piasa Bird
Source: Wikimedia Commons; Author: Theirislion; Title: Piasa
Bird; Date: undated; License: Public Domain; URL:
https://commons.wikimedia.org/wiki/File:PiasaBird.jpg; image
modified for publication

Page 151   Mont Saint-Michel
Source: Wikimedia Commons; Author: trialsanderrors; Title:
Photocrom print by Photoglob Zurich, between 1890 and 1900;
License: Creative Commons Attribution 2.0 Generic; URL:
https://commons.wikimedia.org/wiki/File:Flickr_-
%E2%80%A6trialsanderrors-_North-east_face,_Mont-Saint-
Michel,_Normandy,_France,_ca._1895.jpg; image modified for
publication

Page 162   Newport Tower
Source: Wikimedia Commons; Author: Klsgram; Title: untitled;
Date: 11 March 2012; License: Creative Commons Attribution-
Share Alike 4.0 International; URL:
https://commons.wikimedia.org/wiki/File:Newport_Tower,_RI.j
pg; image modified for publication

Page 175   The Royal Mounds at Gamla Uppsala
Source: Wikimedia Commons; Author: Cyberjunkie; Title: Royal
burial mounds at Old Uppsala at sunset; Date: 10 December 2006;
License: Creative Commons Attriubtion-Share Alike 3.0
Unreported; URL:
https://commons.wikimedia.org/wiki/File:Old_Uppsala_sunset.j
pg; image modified for publication

Page 178   Ramsund Carving

Source: Wikimedia Commons; Author: Richard Dybeck; Title: The
runestone So 101; Date: 1855; License: Public Domain; URL:
https://commons.wikimedia.org/wiki/File:S%C3%B6_101,_Mora.
jpg; image modified for publication

Page 187   Stone ruins, Pukaskwa Pit
Image by Naturally Superior Adventures, used with permission;
image modified for publication

Page 215   Tomb of Saint George the Dragon Slayer
Source: Wikimedia Commons; Author: One ArmedMan; Title: The
tomb of Saint George in Lod, Isreal; License: Public Domain; URL:
https://commons.wikimedia.org/wiki/File:La_tomba_di_San_Gi
orgio_(Lod,_Israele)_02.JPG; image modified for publication

Page 217   Saint Margaret of Antioch
Source: Wikimedia Commons; Author: Antiquary; Title: First
north aisle window, Church of the Good Shepherd, Brighton, East
Sussex. It was designed by Charles Knight and produced by the
firm of Barton, Kinder & Alderson in 1962.; License: Creative
Commons 4.0 Attribution International; URL:
https://commons.wikimedia.org/wiki/File:Good_Shepherd_Chur
ch,_first_north_aisle_window.jpg; image modified for publication

Tomb of Saint George, the Dragon Slayer, located in the
Church of Saint George, Lod, Israel

About the Author

Jake Frost is an attorney and the author of five previous books:

1. *Victory! Poems by Jake Frost*;
2. *From Dust to Stars, Poems by Jake Frost*;
3. *The Happy Jar*, a children's picture book which he also illustrated;
4. *Catholic Dad, (Mostly) Funny Stories of Faith, Family, and Fatherhood*; and
5. *Catholic Dad 2, More (Mostly) Funny Stories of Faith, Family, and Fatherhood*.

He is married with four children.

Saint Margaret of Antioch, from The Church of the Good
Shepherd, Brighton, East Sussex

Made in the USA
Columbia, SC
14 October 2021

46898745R00120